"NO, I THINK THAT I SHALL NOT TELL YOU MY NAME JUST YET," SHE TOYED WITH HIM.

"Then I must give you one," he said. "Perhaps the name of a flower would do well, for your face is as fragile and the rain has touched you with its dew. How to choose from all the flora . . . but I have it. You are the rose. Yes," he told her yet he did not appear to notice her surprise at the uncanniness of his having chosen so accurately. "Lady Rose it shall be, a woman with many adventures— or petals. No other flower has as many petals, except perhaps the mum, but that should not suit you at all for it is brittle and rough and you are delicate and soft. Will you tell me about your other petals?" he asked. "Your other adventures?"

Rosanna was at first too startled by his words to speak. Had she not just compared her life to the very same flower, her intrigues and plans to its petals? How could he have known? She wondered and thought that she would not mind sharing a few of her petals with him. Nor did she doubt he would mind picking off her petals one by one until he reached her heart, such was the look of interest in his eyes . . .

Books by Juliana Davison

The Pink Phaeton
Velvet Ribbons
Petals of The Rose

Published by
WARNER BOOKS

Your Warner Library of Regency Romance

Petals Of The Rose

Juliana Davison

WARNER BOOKS

A Warner Communications Company

WARNER BOOKS EDITION

Copyright © 1980 by Julie Davis
All rights reserved.

Cover art by Walter Popp

Warner Books, Inc., 75 Rockefeller Plaza, New York, N.Y. 10019

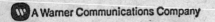 A Warner Communications Company

Printed in the United States of America

First Printing: September, 1980

10 9 8 7 6 5 4 3 2 1

For my father, Ronald
Sometimes stringent, most times supportive
Always loving and loved

Chapter One

All heads turned as Lady Rosanna Shelton entered
the room. Her perfect beauty was admired, often
envied; certainly never unnoticed whether she was
strolling through Hyde Park, taking her seat at the
Opera or now as she was joining her friend, Lady
Christina Chattering, at the Royal Café, the smart
luncheon club whose members each had to be ap-
proved by no less than three peers of the realm.

Rosanna's beauty was distinctly English. Her
black curls framed a clear ivory complexion, graced
still in these warmer months by the blush of a rose,
and those deep red lips were gently parted into a
smile as she caught sight of Christina already seated
at *their* table.

Rosanna's piercing violet eyes scanned the
room for familiar faces, and she was relieved to see
none. She would not wish her lunching alone with

Christina to be taken as a snub by any others in her immediate circle.

"But you do look agitated," Christina said, misinterpreting her friend's behavior. "Do you suspect pursuit? Perhaps we should alert Winston that someone follows at your heels."

"Not at all," Rosanna declined. "That I am being followed is highly unlikely. And were such a drama to unfold, I've no doubt the club's able manservant would not let him cross the red-carpeted boundary."

"But if your pursuer should be the Baronet Playmore, who is a member of this club, and of our circle—so he insists—we shall be undone," Christina teased.

"Are you still convinced he is about to offer his suit?" Rosanna asked.

"Rosanna, how can you doubt it? You are the daughter of an Earl. And while that cannot elevate Lord Playmore's position, it will ensure the birth of a child of nobility," her friend explained.

"This is a fine fix you have landed me in, Christina," she exclaimed playfully. "Not only am I to be saddled with a social bounder for a husband, but with a sadly spoiled child as well—and all in the few minutes that have transpired since my arrival!"

"Of all the ladies in our circle, you are the last I should expect to see saddled in any way," the Lady said, her red curls bouncing as she spoke. "But that does not preclude your taking a husband."

Lady Chattering had done so not three years earlier, only to find herself, presently, a widow at twenty-nine. She was a charming woman and an encouraging friend. Having found the married life unencumbering, she wished Rosanna would try it.

8

Residing in the Earl's house limited the younger girl's prospects for diversion, Christina thought. She wanted Rosanna to be a bit more in the greater stream of life, and the protection of a husband's name, if not title, was all the veil Lady Shelton would need.

"You are correct. I am the only one who has not married," Rosanna remarked in a tone that expressed a hint of regret.

"Why do you delay in joining our ranks?" Christina asked, her blue eyes flashing. "Surely it is not for want of a suitable husband ..."

"That is where you are mistaken," Rosanna said, her hushed voice announcing a confidence. "I doubt I could find a man I would not mind sharing a bed with every night and waking to find beside me on the pillow every morning."

"But you are mistaken," Lady Chattering rejoined. "Nowhere is it written that you must share a common bedchamber nor even a common house. Why Lady Mountharth's husband does not even live in England!"

"Then what indeed is the point of being saddled with the responsibility of a home and husband?" Rosanna asked, her violet eyes widening with curiosity.

"Freedom, my love, that sorely sought human contentment. Marriage, to the proper man, will signify a gain of freedom. Without the cloak of respectability as one's shield, an unmarried will heap all the condemnation for indulging in the same pursuits as a married woman, who will walk with her head held high in any company. If you were married, Rosanna, you would not require even the little protection traveling as a widow affords you," Christina said, still not fully comprehending how

9

she afforded that much to a girl only five years her junior. "If you were a married woman and wished to enjoy the Opera as we will this evening, you might choose Gaylord Pericles as your escort without any hesitation. As it is now, if I were to accept another engagement tonight, you would be forced to sit at home—you could not attend in Gaylord's company alone," she pointed out.

"I should be dreadfully bored in his company without you," Rosanna assured her friend. But she could not help thinking to herself that a marriage of convenience would afford her all she wanted, though it must be said that her doting Papa offered her more liberties and luxuries than any other girl could have dreamed. "He would have to be of the ton, not a drone I would want to hide in the attic," she mused aloud, much to Christina's enjoyment.

"Certainly not," Christina agreed, "though you would have to marry the next Prince of Wales to establish higher allegiance than you now enjoy. But always remember that the principle circumstance is not to lower your social standing, but to strengthen it. One could not err in one's selection of a groom by choosing from Lady Wolverton's circle," she added. She herself had married Lord Chattering, the Earl of Penbrook, a man of sixty who, she thought, had had a great sense of decency by not living far past that advanced age. "Mind you, a man of years is far more accomodating to a young bride who flatters his ego. And yet, I should not recommend your setting your cap for an invalid—that is hardly a thriving existence."

"I think I would also be advised to marry a man younger than my father—for *his* own ego," Rosanna suggested.

"Indeed, that would be highly appropriate,"

Christina agreed. "If you are in accord and wish to pursue the matter, we shall have to bring Lady Wolverton into it. Her experiences will greatly facilitate your path."

"It appears so wholly unnatural that I should not have found one acceptable beau from among those who laid siege at my door after my debut," Rosanna mused. "A beau who would sweep me off my feet and fill my head with every romantic notion ever dreamed by a young girl. Indeed, the men I have met in past years have been exceedingly ignorant, absorbed in their own interests, indifferent to any woman who does not faint dead away at *their* feet."

"Rosanna, you must remember that you have had a singular upbringing. Your father is one of our realm's powerful peers—few *garçons* can hold a candle to him. Your friends are among the most distinguished of society and have made you sophisticated beyond your years—being of less noble birth, this was a lesson I learned only through my marriage. It would be impossible for a man, however handsome and witty, to be provocative and able to compete with those with whom you mingled as a child. That is precisely why you require someone more refined and worldly than a young gadabout. Someone more advanced in years than even the Baronet Playmore, who has avoided any legal entanglement while pursuing the fairest ladies of the town with schemes for seduction foremost in his mind," Christina said, returning to their first subject of conversation, concerning the man who had been calling on Rosanna for upwards of two months without quite succeeding in being invited inside for more than a friendly chat among closely connected acquaintances.

"But the Baronet is well into his fourth decade," Rosanna said. "Surely you do not mean to present me with a man whose birth date is nearly a half century ago!"

"That is precisely what I mean," Christina said. "A bachelor in his forties is after whatever amusement he can find; yet one in his fifties has already come to the conclusion that he will not find as much outside of marriage as he will within its confines. It is an invisible but not ignorable boundary."

"I see," Rosanna said. "There are so many factors to consider . . ."

"But of course," Lady Chattering assured her. "If one were not to take all these considerations into account, one might as well make a runaway match from a suit of passion. But if you wish to find a suitable husband who will afford the most pleasure for the least responsibility, one has to plan the marriage well. If not, you will find yourself with a husband who is totally inappropriate."

As if on cue, the Baronet Playmore joined these two Ladies at their table and said, "Good day, fair enchantresses." He was, Christina thought at that very moment, perhaps the most inappropriate of all the men from whom Rosanna could choose. "What greater fortune can a man hope for in the midst of his day than to encounter two lovelies at his favored luncheon club—and to find them in the throes of a confidence, ears bent one towards the other," he said with a distressing (to the ladies) note of intimacy.

"Surely that will tell you that your presence is less than—" Christina Chattering tried to give him a set-down, but the more gracious Rosanna extended her hand to the gentleman and prevented her friend from committing a *faux pas*.

"I hope my presence does not displease *you*," Playmore said as he took Lady Shelton's hand and brought it to his lips.

"Indeed, your presence does not so much disturb us as it reminds us that we are in a club and not my private sitting room, where our confidences would go unnoticed," Rosanna excused their behavior.

"Yes, though I believe your sitting room to be far more *intime* a setting," he added, intimating he would not mind in the least finding himself there.

"Pray join us," Rosanna offered, indicating to him the vacant chair at their table reserved for just such an occasion.

The Baronet was a tall, portly man, whose fair visage compensated for his imminent baldness. A man of title, though with hardly an inheritance to speak of, he was thought by many to be a fortune hunter when, in fact, he cared not after a woman's financial accounts but was intrigued solely by great beauty and panache. He was not a man who demanded any more luxuries than his title offered him—membership in the Royal Café and a seat at the Exchange. He cared for expensive brandies only when guesting at a wealthy peer's home, for riding when at a friend's estate. He was frequently asked to join an acquaintance at their Opera box, and therefore did not need one of his own—or at their club for a game of whist, and needed only to know how to play well yet lose graciously. Except of course for Peppernell's . . .

It would not be fair fitting to say that he lived merely on the fringe of society or through the indulgences of his friends. He was simply a man who partook of life's diversions when they were offered to him and could certainly—easily—do without them when they were not. The Baronet's greatest passion was for women, and his one tragic flaw was that he had not the money to insure the seduction of most of those he pursued. He had then to rely on a clever wit and cunning tongue, an acute sense of both timing and propriety, all of which so amused the formidable Lady Wolverton that she was persuaded to accept Lord Playmore and make him privy to her set. Though his tastes lay more in the direction of haunting Rosanna than her playful though ofttimes reticent lunching companion, a fact that was evident by the expression of adventure in his eyes as he gazed upon the raven-haired beauty, he had the good sense to divide his attention equally between both women. He was keen enough to realize there was a controlled interest behind Lady Chattering's cold demeanor, and knew that one way not to gain Rosanna's favor would be to incur the wrath of her friend. He was careful not to let his romantic blue-grey eyes linger after Rosanna's path and he frequently redressed himself, indeed forced himself, to look longingly at Christina Chattering. The intrigue of pursuit was what continually kept him turned toward Rosanna; what interest could there be in pursuing the widow, he thought, when he knew he could catch her?

"You are a vision," the Baronet said, addressing himself to Lady Chatterring as he took the seat. "But then black always did become you."

"You forget that my black gown is one of mourning," she reproached him. "My year is not yet done."

"Indeed, I had thought when I saw you last at Lady Wolverton's that it surely must have ... But you were besieged by admirers, ardent suitors all," he said, though thinking to himself that they were, no doubt, suitors, inquiring after the hefty inheritance Lord Chattering had left his young bride. He could not help noticing how well she hid behind the veil of widowhood when it was convenient. He had watched her decline many unpropitious invitations while wearing the black Italian silk. If one's tastes were for the fetching beauty of red curls, one would surely lay claim at Lady Chattering's door, he mused. But now, he thought, he must seek to gain Rosanna's favor and chose to engage Lady Shelton in a roundabout fashion by asking after her father.

"How is the Earl?" the Baronet inquired ever so solicitously. "I can see that his daughter is in the fittest health."

"Father shares in that good health," Rosanna answered, "though I fear he spends far too many hours attending to the duties of his title."

"A stalwart of the realm—we have not enough men of such substance to help us maintain the proper order in this country should our own fools follow the American and French examples and declare their independence," the Baronet said pointedly.

"Had I but known you would follow Madame de Stael's example and hold court at the Café, I should have asked an Oxford man to join us," Lady Chattering said, easily bored with talk of things other than the current fashion rage or gossip of the court.

"Come now, Christina," Rosanna begged her. "If the Baronet accords us the opportunity of opinion, we should not ballyhoo it."

"But I did not intend to invoke your displeasure, yet have succeeded in doing so twice today," he said to Christina in apology. "But you will have no further cause to put a frown on your brow for I must

15

now take my leave. We shall see each other this evening, at the Opera or afterwards at Lady Wolverton's."

"I am happy to learn you are included," Christina began, "I had heard the guest list was quite small."

"Indeed," he replied, ignoring the snub, "I do so prefer intimate affairs." His eyes traveled from Rosanna's eyes to her modest decolletage as he spoke these words, causing the younger lady to blush. "Until this evening," he said and withdrew.

"You needn't have been so castigating, Christina," Rosanna quickly reprimanded her friend.

"Do you now mean to encourage him?" Christina asked, the fringe of a jealousy showing through her smile.

"Not in the least—was it not just a moment ago that we agreed an alliance with the Baronet would have disastrous consequences? I might marry a man I do not like, but not one who likes me and all others of my sex as well," Rosanna insisted, fully aware of Playmore's excesses. "He is amusing, nonetheless."

"Perhaps then you are merely interested in a flirtation?" Christina suggested, hoping to get her friend to admit to any feelings she might have have for the man.

"Not in the least," Rosanna proclaimed once again, not realizing that her answer was a sign for Christina to proceed in that very direction. "He is merely a pet, an excessive flatterer who can be quite charming as well."

The ladies would have to include Mr. Gaylord Pericles in their discussion of the Baronet Playmore if they intended to continue it, for this other gentleman soon took the seat formerly—briefly—occupied by the lord. Mr. Pericles, Lady Chattering's constant companion about town, a man whose interest in *la mode* and gossip was equalled only by his friend Christina's, conspired to allow those of the female sex to regard him as an ally rather than one threatening romantic entanglement.

"Christina, the Italians know how to design for you, my beauty," he said, dropping the formality of addressing her by title. "Such silk and lace—pity it is a mourning robe." He shook his head in disappointment. "But then, if your modiste removes the high neck and the cumbersome sleeves—perhaps then you will have an artful gown for a soiree ... unless you will save it for your next *mari*," he added teasingly.

"I don't know that I will marry again," she confessed. "But you have not yet greeted Rosanna."

"I hope you do not find my musings too out of the ton," he apologized. "It is only that being a widow hardly becomes my dearest Christina."

"No, it does not," Rosanna agreed, not one to be shocked by such candid talk. "In truth, it is all I can do to remember Christina mourns still—but then, the Baronet Playmore was just here to remind us both."

"I saw him as I entered the room and sought to save you both from any prolonged haranguing, but watched him depart as I approached."

"He has a fair sense of timing," Christina muttered.

"And an even keener one for beauty," Gaylord told them in a tone that established his opinion as fact and not flattery.

"Thank you for your kind consideration," Rosanna said.

"A flatterer, yes ... but he was becoming a

dreadful bore," Christina added, protesting a bit too much. "We could hardly talk freely in his presence, and for what should we lunch together if not that?"

"Perhaps I must withdraw as well," Gaylord offered, his pale face searching Christina's for a signal to go or to stay.

"No, no," Christina said. "You should find our conversation amusing at the very least. And if we are fortunate, you will add an anecdote or two as well."

"Then might I tell you about the small soiree I attended last evening?" he asked, and took their smiles as encouragement to continue. "Given by Prince Allessio—that Italian masquerading as royalty, don't you know. Yes, he was in quite a sorry state—and I was quite exhausted by the end of the affair."

"But how was it that we were not included?" Christina asked.

"It was in honor of the latest Italian *emigré* of the Royal Order," he said with a note of sarcasm. "Not one I would insist you invite to your next dinner party. No, no, not influential at all—not like that divine Count Paolo Ertazy. He is a wit, a marvel, but I shan't recount his merits to you now . . . . It has been some time since *you* last threw a bash, has it not?" Gaylord asked.

"Not since Lord Chattering departed," Christina said with a heavy sigh. But only if one listened closely would one know whether the sigh was reserved for Chattering's passing or the lack of diversion.

"I shall help you organize one—for your triumphant return to society," he said, smacking his lips. "We can have it on the anniversary of his death—as a tribute."

"But is it really the thing, Gaylord?" Christina asked, but needing little persuasion.

"Don't be a silly goose—should I let you fall from grace? Never." he insisted with great vehemence, one usually reserved for insuring his hand. "But what of our plans for this evening?"

"Rosanna will be joining us at the Opera and at Lady Wolverton's party *après*. I should like you to have the carriage at my townhouse by eight and we will fetch the dear heart together," Christina said, patting both their hands.

"Delightful!" Gaylord exclaimed, turning from his confidant to Rosanna, a woman whose beauty he judged to be far and away greater than that of any other in the room. He would endeavor, in earnest, to help promote a successful match for the young girl, a passion of his for which he displayed great talent.

Gaylord Pericles was a distant relation of Lady Wolverton, by far the most formidable—and aged!—woman of Rosanna's set. This connection gave him sterling credentials as well as the privilege of unequivocal acceptance despite the fact that he was untitled. He was a confirmed bachelor, not unlike the Baronet Playmore, had as much of a penchant for the company of women, hardly for the same reasons, but chiefly for luncheon and Opera soirees. He preferred to be an escort and friend rather than a potential husband or seducer. When one was with Gaylord, one could trust him implicitly. It was only unfortunate, he thought, that Rosanna was not protected by the veil of matrimony, for he should have liked to become one of her intimates, accepted in her immediate circle. Her father was a very powerful man, one he wished to know.

Mr. Pericles had not the advantage of masculine beauty. His complexion was chalky, worse than pale, and his light eyes did little to brighten his visage. But his qualities were endearing—his gentle understanding of many female emotions, for one, and he could be depended on to render an honest opinion from the male vantage point on a variety of subjects and situations, from the judging of the comeliness of a dress to the wording of a love note to the most appropriate way to set down a suitor. He was considered an asset in one's drawer of friends, to Lady Chattering especially as she had begun to reassemble her life so many months after the death of her husband, a grief Gaylord and, more recently Rosanna, had come to understand. Though there was no passion in her marriage, there was a great fondness in Christina's heart followed by a sadness at his passing, a disconsolation all her new-found admirers could not fully repair, one her gay countenance often kept hidden.

The trio partook of their usual luncheon, stopping after each mouthful to exchange a tale or two concerning mutual acquaintances. Rosanna would have liked to fritter away the afternoon, languishing until the tea hour approached and continuing the merriment through 'til sunset, but she had to return to her home on Curzon Street and now begged to be excused.

"I must speak with Father before the Opera," she confessed.

"Rosanna, darling, you must seriously consider giving up your life as a daughter for one of a wife," Christina reiterated. "A suitable mate is what you are sorely lacking."

"Do you mean by suitable a man I might easily discard after the ceremony?"

Christina did not answer. She merely lowered her eyes and smiled.

"I will take it under advisement, dear friend. Perhaps it is the wisest course for me to take. After all, I shouldn't wish to pass by any of the delights marriage can offer ... save for one," she added with a wicked smile. She kissed her friend below her demi-veil and swept through the room much as she had entered it, with all heads turned to watch her.

Chapter Two

"Rosanna, when will you stop associating with that *widow*?" It was becoming her father's preferred salutation, one whose meaning remained the same whether he varied it with "Where have you been?" or "Why are you tearing at my heart so?"

Though she had thought to reply, on certain occasions, to the last with, "Father, I was not aware you still had your heart," then and now, she bit her lip instead and offered, "How can you be so disparaging towards the wife of one of your dearest friends?"

"My dear, *departed* friend . . . I am certain that woman had a hand in sending poor Egbert into the next world," he insisted.

"Father, that is one of the most shocking thoughts I have ever heard! Christina loved Lord Chattering and he in turn loved her. How can you condemn her simply because he is no longer with us? Can't you respect his choice in a wife?" Rosanna asked.

"In a word—no!" said the Earl, but would not be content with a mere syllable. "I am convinced that his choosing her at such a late date was the work of senility knocking at his front door. And Egbert, good-natured soul that he was, let her in," the Earl contended. "Rosanna, I am sure that your friend is a very charming and clever woman, but the fact remains that she is of humble birth and would not be traveling in our circles had it not been for her marriage to Lord Chattering. She is a fortune seeker, perhaps not of the worst kind, but a fortune seeker nonetheless. Though it would not be possible to take from her all the gains her marriage brought her, that does not mean her standing is secure, and she seeks now to benefit from an acquaintance such as yours."

"Which of my other acquaintances do you prefer? I do believe you would find fault with one and all," his daughter suggested.

"Nonsense, Rosanna. It is just that you spend so much of your time with Lady Chattering, whom I do not feel can benefit you in any way," her father said with calmer demeanor.

"And what of Lady Irva Wolverton?"

"That old bag!" Lord Shelton said before realizing he had fallen snugly into his clever offspring's trap. "Do not look at me with those eyes .... I speak the truth," he protested.

"You would not have a *bon mot* for any of my friends—just as you did not for any of the suitors who came to call on me," she said in an angry voice. But then she realized, as always, that her father's remarks stemmed from honorable reasoning—that he wanted only the best for his child. Her rigid posture softened as she stepped forward to put her arms around his neck. "Father, I love and respect you. I seek your guidance and direction at every turn in my life. But you must recognize that there comes a time when you must begin to worry a little less about me. I have long since past my come-out, I am not the little girl you and Grandmama had to raise without benefit of my mother. You fretted twice as much—as a father and as a mother. You offered twice the encouragement, and—it must be said—twice the reproach when you disagreed with me, to compensate for the unfillable void Mama's death left in our lives. With all that, you have given me a stubborn will. Just as you let nothing ill befall me as a child, I shall prevent such an occurrence in the future and you must endeavor to cool your passion on the subject of my friends whom you do not admire.

"I fully realize it is impossible to ask you to like Christina, but you must try to make life a bit less impossible for me as I continue to reside in this house." Rosanna looked up at her father, awaiting his reply.

Arthur Shelton, the Earl of Severn, was a tall, portly man with a pleasing face and a ruddy complexion. His hair was now completely grey, perfectly attributable to the years of worry following Rosanna's come-out, he would tell her. His large eyes were clear blue; they radiated all of the concern he felt in his heart for his only chid. He was a handsome man who had caught the eye of many a widow, without effort. Though many of these hoped to win his affection, none could hope to take Rosanna's place in his heart.

Lila, the Countess of Severn, had died at the

tragically early age of thirty, leaving a man who loved her more than life itself and a daughter of ten who had inherited all her sultry beauty and charming ways. It was then that the Earl enlisted his mother-in-law in the raising of this child. In the fifteen years since, he and Lady Dorothy Simpson had maintained Lila's beloved Curzon Street townhouse and had raised the beauty who now stood in the Earl's library.

Lord Shelton openly admitted that he was stubborn-willed, a trait he had involuntarily passed on to his daughter. In deciding an issue with two distinct answers, he did not have any inclination to consider the side he had not chosen, a flaw in his character made more evident by the fact that his mother-in-law invariably adopted the opposing viewpoint: be it on the subject of politics (which Lady Simpson had learned since living in the Earl's house), of domestics (in which she had endeavored to school her son-in-law) or of Rosanna whom both were willing to place before all other concerns, including the Earl's not inconsiderable Parliamentary responsibilities.

"Rosanna," he said, taking a step backwards to look more forcibly into her eyes, "it is only when I see you caught between the attentions of that widow and a beau like the Baronet—what is his name, Playmore?—that I wonder what will become of you when I am gone."

"Father, I cannot deliberate Christina's merits as a friend with you anymore, but you can rest assured that the Baronet and I will never be anything more than the most casual of acquaintances. His manner is artful, his conversation charming, even witty at times, but I beseech you to remember that on the numerous occasions he had left his card

25

with Alcott, our cherished butler, he has never been invited indoors nor been given the slightest encouragement. Why even today, when he joined Christina and me at the Café—"

"You and that widow allowed him to sit between the two of you?" he asked, his eyebrows knotting together in a frown. "I cannot believe it! You had him join you as though he were one of your intimates—it is the outside of enough!"

"Father, you pay no attention to the point I am trying to introduce!" Rosanna implored him to listen.

"Rosanna, your having accepted his company is all that I needed to hear . . ."

"But we were at the Café. Surely you would not have had us let him linger, bent over our shoulders like a servant or a lollygag!?"

"I am certain all heads were turned in your direction from the start—a widow still in her blacks at a luncheon spot such as the Café. Oh, daughter!" he moaned. "Can you not remember your birth?"

"Father, you prove the verity of my earlier words. No friend of mine will ever be of noble enough birth nor high enough social standing to satisfy you," Rosanna said and sighed.

"What do you mean to say, Rosanna?" the Earl asked.

"Simply that I might as well choose my associates, indeed even the man to whom I should be betrothed, as I will for you shall always find displeasure in the company I keep!" she exclaimed.

"If you persist in that tone, daughter, I shall be forced to admit I no longer tolerate you either," he said coldly.

"You need not worry on that score, Father, for I will leave you at once. This altercation affords me no pleasure," she said, her anger burning hotly in her cheeks. She turned on her heels and left the room.

Rosanna Shelton was a sweet-natured girl who thought of everyone's comfort before her own. But when her feathers were ruffled, her back arched like a cat threatened and there was no remedy save retreat. Rosanna walked the length of the second floor corridor toward her chamber when she thought she would prefer to seek solace in her grandmother's sitting room.

Grandmother Dorothy was knitting an infant's sweater when Rosanna discovered her. She had been knitting infant sweaters since the girl's come-out. Lady Simpson would be prepared when Rosanna made her a great grandmother. She would not be taken by surprise. Dorothy Simpson was a spry woman for her age, which was eighty-three, one who was determined to make up for the loss of her daughter through the gain of her granddaughter and Rosanna's heirs. She vowed she would not quit this earth until she saw her great grandchild and that when she did, the wool blankets and sweaters and caps and mittens would form part of the legacy she left behind.

Her face was, as only fitting for a grandmama, slightly pudgy, with rounded, rosy cheeks and a cherubic smile. Her white hair was swept into a chignon, a fashion she had worn since her youth. When uncoiled, her tresses hung about her waist, silver strands spun of silk so soft and graceful, Rosanna thought on those rare occasions when she was allowed to braid it. As a child, Rosanna was easily put in a pout that her hair was never as long or as fine as her grandmother's, but she would have her nanny braid and coil it just the same. Imitation was never a more sincere form of flattery, and the desire to be like her grandmother in every way was ever obvious in Rosanna's eyes.

"Have you and Arthur been arguing again?" Lady Simpson asked without lifting her eyes from her work.

"Indeed, again and again ... will it ever cease?" Rosanna asked.

"How can it?" Grandmother replied. "In the years since your father and I have been living in this unconventional fashion, our bickerings have reached a finely-honed perfection. Give it more time and yours will as well," she promised. "Some people are destined to argue and others need never speak a word to know their feelings are shared. Has my son-in-law the good taste to banter on a new topic or does he still harp on your friendship with the lovely Lady Chattering?"

One look at her granddaughter's expression gave her the answer. "It is an issue you will never resolve with him," Lady Simpson continued. "Not even if he were to marry her himself .... But perhaps if we could entertain a small dinner party so that he might get to know her better?"

"Could we?" Rosanna asked, coming to life.

"We could invite twenty guests—anything larger would be highly inappropriate for then we should be inviting less than our peers," Grandmama said, ever willing to further Rosanna's education in the customs of etiquette.

"I doubt it would have the desired effect. Father became well-acquainted with Christina during her marriage, but did not like her from the first. He has not altered his opinion of her in the least. But this is a perfect excuse to plan the soiree, and I am of complete accord. It is truly inspirational . . . . Too many months have passed since the festivities of the winter season and we have been sorely lacking in diversion. Might we set to work on it at once?" she asked.

"Alcott will see to the tedious details as usual," her grandmother assured her.

"I should like to help in the planning of the menu," Rosanna said, "as I shall be responsible for such details when I command a home of my own."

"That is unique talk coming from you, grandchild. Have you settled on a husband as well?"

"Not yet," Rosanna assured her. "But we can say that I am keeping a close watch for a suitable one."

"If I were you, young lady, I should hire a matchmaker to watch while you sleep. It will be no less than a miracle for you to find a *suitable* husband. I would venture to say that it is an impossibility. The most one can hope for is a mate one can, at best, tolerate. As long as there are men and women, there will be differences between them and subjects on which they will never see eye to eye.

"I loved Oscar—may he rest in peace—but suited to each other? We were not well-suited in the least. Do not be concerned with suitability—it is the impossible quest. Settle on someone who will not interfere with you and whom you will not have to watch over too closely. Therein lies sustained happiness," Lady Simpson promised.

"But what of passion and romance?" Rosanna asked.

"They are pleasing to the heart of a young girl, but passion soon cools and romance wanes with a courtship's progression. Only a deeper understanding and rational communication can insure happiness with the man whom you take as a husband," Lady Simpson told her.

"Was there a passion between you and Grandfather Oscar?" Rosanna asked.

"The very problem with passion," Lady Simpson answered in the stringent voice she used when she wished her words to make a lasting impression, "is that it does not last. And if one gets accustomed to it from the start, one will begin to miss it with aching—tis not worth the effort to regret its early passing."

Rosanna was not surprised by her grandmother's theory. It confirmed her own thoughts, and that saddened her only by its finality. She had wanted almost to be talked out of her carefully planned scheme of a marriage of convenience. But now found herself further convinced of the logic in Christina's suggestion.

Rosanna became so obssessed by these thoughts that when she found herself in the drawing room an hour later, in the company of both her elders, all three sipping hot tea, she did not at first realize they were arguing, and about her nonetheless. But soon their voices burgeoned from a buzz to a full symphony.

"Do you mean I am to suffer the company of that Lady Chatterbox?" the Earl bellowed.

"Do you deem that the best tone to use when you are addressing the mother of your departed wife?" Grandmama asked, not one to ignore the device of a guilt-inspiring tone.

"I need not you to remind me of my continued devotion to the memory of my darling Lila," the Earl said in a tone completely out of character with his proper, official demeanor. If anything could cause him to shirk that stance it was talk of Lila, or his daughter and her future. Though he had tried to these past fifteen years to conquer the foe he found in his equally beloved mother-in-law, he had not succeeded.

Lord Shelton kept a level head even when enraged in battle with Rosanna, whose warring skills were kept sharpened, but he could not maintain his equilibruim vis-a-vis the white-haired woman over whom he towered by no less than a foot. There was perhaps something in her diminutive size which unnerved him greatly even as it instilled in her a superior presence that caused her to dominate everyone who came into view—even if she would have been forced to stand on a chair to face her adversary eye-to-eye.

"I wish you would stop your fighting for the course of at least one meal," Rosanna said, her head coming out of the clouds. "Perhaps if there were not so much quibbling going on in my home I would not seek to absent myself from it with such frequency."

Rosanna succeeded in silencing both, but as soon as she finished her mint tea, quit them to begin her toilette.

As her abigail Betty styled her hair, Rosanna thought of how often she felt she lived in two different worlds; the one of her friends, like Christina, where she was treated as an individual with feelings and opinions and thoughts of interest to all, and the one of her family, however limited, where she became the daughter and the granddaughter, the constant subject of bickering, less of a person and more of a dilemma that had to be solved. Even if they were to accord her the privileges they enjoyed, she thought, she would have nary the time to use them, always being called upon to stay their enraged arguments, to keep each from hurting the other.

Marrying, she was convinced, would solve not only her search for independence, but would put a welcomed period on their tenuous relationship.

Rosanna stepped into the beige *peau de soie* dress, a gown she appreciated for its modest decollete and its lace-trimmed sleeves, and stood silently pondering her fate, while Betty did the row of thirty pearl buttons that began at the small of her mistress's back and extended upwards to the nape of her long neck.

Rosanna determined to seek out all prospects, save the youngsters, as she thought them, who attempted to leave their card with Alcott or gain introduction through a mutual friend. That species of man would not do at all. She had no qualms about initiating an acqaintance with a man of the proper age and breeding to fill her needs. She doubted that any such man would venture into her domain without prompting, placing himself out of her youthful league, not willing to suffer the possible humiliation of being scorned by one of her tender years and advanced beauty. And any old fool who did more than attempt to draw her eyes in his direction and exchange a brief smile was not the man for her.

The opera house at Covent Garden was a scene of gaiety, a blaze of light. Rosanna, in her ermine-trimmed cape, worn more for impression than necessity on this temperate April evening, shined no less brightly, flanked on either side by Lady Christina Chattering and Mr. Gaylord Pericles. She moved like quicksilver towards her friend's box. Lord Chattering had taken it for his wife the year before his death; neither he nor his trusted friend, Lord Shelton, had much cared for the music, but Egbert knew it would please Christina, the rationale he used for most of the unusual decisions he made in the last stages of his life (the reason his friend, the Earl, took a dislike to the woman he regarded as manipulative and calculating).

"What piece do we see this evening?" Rosanna asked Mr. Pericles.

"A recent offering by the Italian, Gioacchino Rossini. *Il Barbiere di Siviglia,*" he answered.

"*The Barber of Seville,*" Christina offered the English translation. "I have not yet read the libretto, but it promises to be quite amusing."

"I wonder that you will see parallels to your own life, my darling," Gaylord said to her. "It received most negative criticism when it opened two years ago in Rome." He turned to Rosanna and said, "But tonight we are to have the honor of hearing none other than Manuel Garcia—of Seville, no less."

"I am sure we will all be enchanted by the virtuoso," Lady Chattering assured her guests, she herself more entranced by being at the Opera than seeing the opera itself.

Rosanna, too, was excited at finding herself at Covent Garden. It had been far too long an interval for one so keenly interested in the art. The music, the delightful scenery, the intricately worked costumes and the power within the talented performers always combined to create a most magical feeling in the air. But when the manager of the company appeared on the stage, a hush fell over the buzzing theater. The disappointing news was that Mr. Garcia would not be able to sing that evening; his understudy would endeavor to replace him and another presentation arranged.

33

"It is an outrage," Mr. Pericles insisted and suggested they quit Convent Garden at once rather than suffer an inferior performance.

Rosanna and her friend pleaded with him to stay.

"Perhaps this way we will acquire an understanding of the story which will better enable us to appreciate Señor Garcia's performance at a later date," Rosanna reasoned with him.

"If *you* do not mind, dear lady," Mr. Pericles acquiesed and took his seat again.

The performance proved satisfactory, but, for a reason unknown to Rosanna, left Christina quite disturbed by the time of its conclusion.

"What did Gaylord mean when he suggested the piece might reflect your life?" Rosanna asked, hoping to understand her friend's discomfiture.

"I have no inkling," Christina answered in a measured tone," "for I have never been in love with a handsome and virile young man whom I was forbidden to marry. I would not have let my father's protests stop me as it did the heroine, and for fully three-quarters of the piece!" she most vehemently denied any similarity.

"I am certain that my father would oppose both suitors," Rosanna stated. "And so I find little reflection of my own existence. I am now convinced to do precisely as you suggested, Christina," Rosanna intimated at her search for a husband of respected years.

Here Christina's expression changed dramatically. "Perhaps it was a suggestion offered in haste. Perhaps you are not in need of an older husband after all."

"But what of the advantages it brought you?"

Rosanna reminded her, confused by her friend's change of attitude.

"It can prove to be more confining than I led you to believe," she said and appeared to be on the brink of a confidence, but something held her back. She saw the distraught look on Rosanna's face and sought to end the conversation by saying simply, "You must evaluate your situation carefully and make the choice that suits you the best."

"Shall we press forward to Lady Wolverton's?" Mr. Pericles suggested, wholly disinterested by what Christina had *almost* said.

"I think I must forgo Lady Wolverton's this evening," Lady Chattering replied. "I am feeling out of sorts."

"Will you accompany me?" the escort asked Lady Rosanna Shelton.

"I am afraid that would be impossible," Rosanna declined. "I must ask that you both take me home presently."

Rosanna was now as dejected as Christina for she had been greatly anticipating the party at her most illustrious friend's apartment, and knew that her maidenhood was what kept her from attending on Gaylord's arm.

When she arrived at Curzon Street, her father's greeting added pain to her disappointment.

"How come you are home at such an early hour? Was not Lady She-wolf's party of interest to you?"

"Come now, Arthur," Grandmother Dorothy hushed him, never lifting her eyes from her needlework. "Good-night, darling," she called to Rosanna as she heard the girl's foot alight on the stair.

"Good-night," Rosanna called back, but not until she reached the upstairs landing. She quickly entered her room and threw herself down upon her bed.

"Can I be of assistance?" Betty, a perceptive miss of seventeen, asked.

Rosanna stood and let the girl help her from her gown into her bed-dress. But there was little other remedy for Lady Shelton that evening. As she put her head down on her pillow, she closed her eyes, but could not erase all thought from her mind. She was annoyed that she had been denied Lady Wolverton's party; she was concerned after her friend Christina's bizarre reaction to the opera, and she was disappointed with herself that she had not, in the years since her come-out, improved her own life in any way. She never had had any use for the affections of a suitor and always thought she was still of that opinion. But now that she had come to fully realize the advantages of a husband, she made up her mind to begin her quest in earnest that weekend when she would be at Lady Wolverton's hunting party, an invitation which made up for this evening's loss.

As she snuffed the candle at her night table, her one unresolved question concerned her friend. What had overtaken Christina Chattering? she wondered again. *Perhaps it is all in my imagination*, she said aloud. After all, Gaylord Pericles did not appear to take the slightest interest in his friend's foul mood and he was a man whose love of gossip and confidences far surpassed that of any other mortal.... But upon further reflection, Rosanna understood this to mean one thing alone: that Gaylord shared the secret of Christina's thoughts. Rosanna's curiosity was piqued. She would not be satisfied until she knew what *II Barbière* had said to provide such a change in her friend. She endeavored to find this out at the earliest opportunity, but not before her dreams invaded with faceless men all in a row.

Chapter Three

"Well, it is the most exciting news I have heard today," Lady Wolverton said, though she realized this gave little indication of her excitement, the hour being just past ten in the morning. "But who is the lucky groom?"

"Dear lady, that is where the main problem lies. I have not yet settled on one," Rosanna explained.

"That does put a crimp in the scheme, does it not?" Irva Wolverton replied. "But not to worry— by the end of your country sojourn, I will have selected the most appropriate candidate for you," she promised with anticipation. "Create him if need be. But now we must return to the others, for surely they must wonder if I show you every nook this manse has to offer."

Actually, Lady Wolverton's mansion of thirty

rooms had barely been uncovered to Rosanna. Indeed, apart from showing her the guest room on the second floor which Rosanna was to occupy, they had barely left the parlor floor. It would have taken upwards of an hour to have given the most peripheral peek to each of the magnificently furnished suites of the High Wycombe estate.

Rosanna had made Lady Wolverton's acquaintance late the previous summer and the cold winter months had made this journey from London a perilous one. This was her first visit to the hundred acre sprawl west of the capital. She would not have been able to make this visit now were it not for her Grandmother who accepted the invitation on both their behalves. One can be sure that the Earl of Severn declined such illustrious company, on the occasion of a parliamentary crisis. But Lady Simpson had been easily persuaded to attend. Her acceptance had caused quite a rift between her and her son-in-law, but she was not one to let that kind of altercation sway her.

When Lady Wolverton and Rosanna returned to the drawing room, Lady Alana Quentin and her betrothed, Lord Darnley, were sipping sherry with Lord Wolverton and appeared not to notice the others' return. Alana had a bored look on her face as she watched Eliot, her fiancé, as he was soundly beaten by her stepfather from the very outset of the game of whist. Alana was Irva Wolverton's daughter from her first marriage to Berger Quentin, the Duke of Warringrook. He died in his early forties, and without seeing his daughter wed. Indeed, his widow took her second husband before Alana herself was affianced, at the age of thirty-two, to the very dashing, if somewhat impoverished, Viscount Darnley.

39

Alana's cousin, Lady Celeste Beaufort, arrived soon after in the company of her suitor, the handsome Mr. Ashton Heal, a neighbor of the Wolverton's.

"Who else will be joining us?" Celeste asked, her blond curls bouncing upon the top of her head as she spoke in animated tones.

"Christina Chattering, of course, and our distant relation, Gaylord Pericles," Lady Wolverton said, counting them off on the beringed fingers of her right hand. "Oh yes, and the Baronet Playmore who succeeded in extracting an invitation while at our London apartments earlier in the week."

"What bit of mischief did he promised in exchange?" her auburn-haired daughter asked. "Has he tempted you with the plans of some new scheme or a secret he has learned elsewhere?"

"Never you mind, child," her mother warned. "Lord Darnley will have his hands full with you," she teased. Irva Wolverton was, in truth, grateful that her daughter had finally settled on one of her suitors. The girl was too beautiful and too rich to escape the embarrassment of a ruined reputation much longer.

"Why do you bother him, Aunt? He is not one of us—his tastes are so . . ." Celeste searched for the correct word.

"Common," Mr. Heal said to her.

"Indeed, Mama," Alana said, "though I must admit his conversation is witty—"

"In an odd sort of way," her betrothed finished the sentence.

"I have forgotten that my own brother, Gregory Waltham, will be joining us as well," Lady Wolverton said, looking at Rosanna. "You have not yet made his acquaintance."

"No, I have not," the girl answered, piqued.

"I think you will be intrigued by him," the hostess added.

For the first time since her arrival, Dorothy Simpson looked up from her knitting towards the handsome visàge of her hostess, her junior by no more than twenty years. She wondered if there was any significance behind Irva's last statement. She hoped that Gregory Waltham was her *younger* brother.

Day turned quickly to evening, and with the hunt to begin at six the next morning, Lady Wolverton decided they would wait no longer for the others to arrive before they supped. The cook would be easily persuaded to prepare a cold collation for the travelers who arrived later in the night.

"But it is not fair that we will get more repose than the others," Celeste said innocently.

"It is time you learned, girl," her aunt told her, "that all is not fair in this world. Tomorrow, the fox will not think this world a fair place, but that will not stop *us*, will it?"

Beware to all those foxes in men's clothing, Rosanna thought to herself, for on the morrow her own hunt would begin as well.

As she and her grandmother ascended to their adjoining rooms, Lady Simpson turned to the young girl and asked, "Are you enjoying yourself?"

"Yes, Grandmother. Why do you doubt it?"

"Perhaps it is that I am older and less patient. But child, tell me, do you not find your friends a trifle dull? They are overly concerned with maintaining a level of being that few others can share. As well you know, I would never encourage you to associate with any common types, but I should not like to think that we raised you to be so stringent in *your* choice of friends," Lady Simpson whispered though they now stood within their sitting room.

"I agree that, at first, they might seem cold and preoccupied with maintaining a certain order in their lives, but as you get to know them... they don't often make new acquaintances, preferring to limit themselves to family and a handful of others. You like Christina, don't you?" Rosanna asked, needing to hear a voice of approval and not knowing how to better explain her other friends whose introduction was made through Mr. Pericles.

"But Christina is such a delightful young woman, so charming and full of spirit. Lady Wolverton, though powerful and well-to-do, seems the slightest bit distant; she has built herself a small principality and garners her friends at her bosom, letting the rest of the world and its circumstances fall asunder."

"Those are harsh impressions to be taken from a first meeting," Rosanna said, but without reproach.

"I will wait until our stay is over to say more," Lady Simpson offered, not wishing Rosanna to think she had been cleaved from the same stone block as the Earl of Severn.

"Good-night then," Rosanna said and kissed her cheek.

"Enjoy yourself at the hunt," Lady Simpson said, patting the girl's hand.

"You will not come with us?" her granddaughter teased, knowing full well that Lady Simpson would never participate in such an event.

"I will wait for you at the house," her grandmother answered. "And my prayers are with the little fox!"

When Rosanna caught sight of the furry grey creature caged at the start of the Wolverton fox trail, her heart sank. She looked into its little black eyes and doubted she could go through with the chase. Nevertheless, she climbed atop her horse and adjusted the brown cap that held her long black tresses inside its dome. She seized the reins and waited for the other members of the hunting party to assemble.

The dress was traditionally formal. Red coat over a white high-collared sweater and tan riding breeches tucked into the finest calf boots. It would be difficult to tell the men from the women, Rosanna had thought as she watched Betty tuck her glorious mane of hair from view. But now she realized that the hunting uniform would adequately keep her hair from flying in her face as she chased after her quarry. She was soon joined on the trail by Christina Chattering. "You must have arrived well into the night, for it was nine when we took to bed," Rosanna told her.

"Poor Gaylord had a horrendous time of it getting here. He and the coachman had a tiff over which road to take out of London, the rains having muddied even the broadest thoroughfares. I am surprised our hosts have not called off the hunt," Christina said.

"A true huntsman does not let inclement weather stand in his way," Rosanna insisted, raising her fist high into the air in a sign of mock heroism.

"Humph!" was her friend's reply. Were she not trying to cotton to Gaylord's relations, she would be snug in her bed at this unfathomable hour, Christina thought to herself.

"Did you know that the Baronet Playmore will be among us?" Rosanna so informed her friend and was not unaware of the expression that overtook Christina's face, one that could only be described as amused. "But I have not seen him this morning. If he did not arrive before you and Gaylord, there is little likelihood in his joining us for the hunt."

"Unless the demons keep him from sleep during the night," Christina commented wryly.

The others were soon upon them, their horses biting at their respective bits, eager to cover the countryside, bred for this pursuit alone. They amassed on the side of the trail while Sir Edmund Thurbell, Master of the Fox Hounds, led the whippers-in to the start. These liveried aides of Sir Thurbell gathered together the pack of hounds around the fox's cage. They were hungry beasts, their tongues panting mercilessly in front of their prey.

The coverts were drawn and the members of the party were warned to prepare themselves as Lord Wolverton sounded his horn. The fox was set free and quickly disappeared into the forest ahead, the hounds tearing after him at a no less fervent pace.

It was obvious from the first that Lord Wolverton was the only one in the party taking the hunt seriously. Lady Quentin and her cousin Celeste, giggled as the horses charged and shook them up and down in the saddle.

"Come along, ladies!" Lady Wolverton cried out as she followed her husband. "We must not let Lord Wolverton take the brush without a fight."

Rosanna and Christina, trailing behind the others, soon became aware of the crackling sound at their heels. They turned their heads in unison to see the Baronet Playmore galloping on a great stallion, hoping to overtake them.

"Good morning, Ladies," he called out, assuming they would slow their pace—which they did not, compelling him to increase his.

"Have you just arrived from London?" Christina asked.

"Surely you do not think that I sported my riding outfit through the streets of our capital and the outlying towns, Lady Chattering," he answered, not put off by the affront.

"I do believe my friend was trying to be amusing," Rosanna said, easing the tension in the crisp morning air.

"Tis too early to hope for that," Playmore said. "If the truth be known, I am not well used to rising at such an hour and did oversleep."

"I am sure that your bedchamber habits are of little business ours," Christina retorted.

"Indeed . . . I merely explain—I am simply glad that I have not missed the whole of the hunt," he said, stumbling over his words. He had never let a woman trip him in such a fashion, he thought to himself. Why now? And in front of Lady Shelton, the fair Rosanna . . .

"Quite to the contrary," Christina assured him. "You have caught up with its keenest participants."

"But where is the fox?" he asked, unaware that in her own private hunt, he was Lady Chattering's quarry.

"Ahead, I suspect," Rosanna answered his question. "Unless he is more clever than we thought, and has run 'round to hide about us where he knows he must be safe."

"The Wolvertons keep a nasty pack of hounds. I should stay away from them were I the hunted," the Baronet said, his horse's pace slowing now that he might ride abreast with the ladies. "When I arrived late last night, at near two in the morning, they did make a horrible fracas outside the south gate. I was certain all in the manor house would be awakened."

"On that, you need have no qualms," Christina rejoined. "Despite your arrival, we did all sleep quite snugly." She looked from him to Rosanna and entreated her to join the others. "Come, Rosanna, or they will wonder what has become of us." And Lady Chattering's horse leaped forward under the jolt of her riding crop. She was sure Rosanna would follow at her heels.

Much to both Ladies' surprise, fate was leading Rosanna in another direction.

Rosanna tried to gain some momentum, but the Baronet's horse inched ahead of her and seemed to purposefully nuzzle her horse off the trail.

"Lord Playmore, I wish you would control the beast. This is hardly fitting," she exclaimed, taken by surprise.

"I must tell you, dear beauty, that the horse is completely in my control, and soon, you will be as well."

"I do not understand," Rosanna said, raising her voice. "What can you mean by this monstrous behavior?"

"Dear lady, can it be that you have never before been part of a scheme of seduction?" he asked blatantly.

"Is that what this is, Lord Playmore?" Rosanna asked, her voice becoming slightly more shrill.

"Indeed," he assured her as both horses were led deeper into the forest.

He had seized her reins from her, but their pace slowed as the forest became more dense, trees and shrubs prohibiting further passage. He drew the horses to a halt. He slid from his saddle towards Rosanna, hoping to extract what he hoped would be a welcomed kiss. Still holding both sets of reins, he walked around to her. He extended his free hand and she panicked, not knowing how to escape him.

An idea sprang to mind, not an artful plan, she thought, completely savage in fact, but the only one she could think of.

"I am afraid that your adventure has left me quite frozen in the saddle. I need the strong assistance of both your hands to help me down," she said, all the while trying not to laugh.

The Baronet was very willing to believe that Rosanna desired him as much as he did her, and was quick to drop the reins and hold his hands outstretched. She held her hands open so as to entice him into moving closer. As the slim begloved hands distracted him, Rosanna's pointed boot toe aimed at the Lord's midsection. With a push of all her might, she sent him sprawling to the ground, mud splattering all over his white breeches.

"You shall have to concoct an artful tale to explain this tragedy," Rosanna called merrily, "unless you are willing to admit that you are so not clever a huntsman as you claim." There was mockery in her voice that she did not even think to check, so enraged was she at his behavior.

"Come back, my beauty, my raven-haired vixen," Playmore cried out, not realizing how comic a sight he presented, in mud up to his knees.

Rosanna answered his plea with the most coquettish of laughter that echoed through the branches along with the brisk clapping of her horse's hooves.

At first Rosanna was confused by all the different paths the forest offered. But she looked into the sky for a patch of blue signaling a clearing. When she found the fox trail, she realized she had left the forest at a point closer to the manor house than where she and Lord Playmore had entered. She doubted she could catch the others and decided to return to the house. It would be easy enough to explain that a headache had forced her back, and let the Baronet contrive whatever excuse he would. She was certain he would corroborate any tale she chose to spin, rather than risk having his humiliating failure known to all. A scheme for seduction! She laughed aloud at the thought and wondered how she might have been the least bit frightened.

Rosanna left her horse with the stableboy, who was confused by her early return. She felt grateful for being able to take off her cap and let her curls tumble freely about her shoulders. She could not have known how becoming a sight she was, what with the blush of her mishap with Playmore still on her cheeks.

When Count Gregory Waltham espied her as she approached the patio where he was seated, enjoying a cup of tea and the morning papers, he could not quite account for his good fortune.

Chapter Four

"You appear to have as deep an appreciation for the hunt as I," Lord Waltham said wryly.

"I have developed a headache ... from all the sounding of horns," Rosanna explained, her hands making a spiral towards the sky to imitate the loud notes.

"You might find comfort in knowing that your discomfiture has not marred your beauty in the least," he said.

"I think it only fair fitting to know the name of the person who offers such a compliment," Rosanna said without offering the secret of her own identity.

"I am Gregory Waltham, Lady Wolverton's brother," he told her.

Rosanna's eyes widened upon hearing his name. She took in more fully the portrait he presented. He was a tall, slim man with silver hair and grey eyes that often changed to blue. His complexion was healthy from vigorous activity perhaps, though not equestrian exercise. Rosanna was certain he was at least her father's age, any more years were concealed by his slender form.

Lord Waltham wore a deep blue velvet morning coat and a pair of grey trousers, a white ascot tied distinctively about his throat. A handsome portrait, Rosanna thought, and saw not his age, but the wisdom behind his eyes and an interest there as well.

"But you have not yet told me who you are," he continued and extended a hand to her.

"Rosanna Shelton," she said and offered her hand.

"Lady Shelton, daughter of the Earl of Severn?"

"Do you know my father?"

"Indeed. We have met in London over business affairs. I knew he had a daughter, but suspected she was much younger," he said and left Rosanna hoping that she appeared quite mature for her tender years.

"I am glad that we have met now. Your sister was anxious for me to make your acquaintance. She thought we might have much in common—a love of the Opera, for instance," Rosanna suggested.

"Were you at Covent Garden for the disappointing presentation of *Il Barbiere?*"

"Yes," Rosanna replied, "but I have not yet formed a conclusive opinion on the piece. I am waiting to hear Señor Garcia perform—it was a terrible disappointment that he fell ill."

"Then you must ask your fiancé to take you as

soon as the presentation is announced," he remarked.

"My fiancé?" Rosanna asked, thinking perhaps she had not heard him correctly. "I have none."

"But I was under the impression that every beautiful lady of London who was not married was, at the very least, betrothed," he said, making her blush.

"I have not been so fortunate as to find an appropriate fiancé," she confessed and held her hands nervously at her sides.

"Would you think me forward if I should ask why?"

"Not forward, but forthright," she replied. "Without seeming to appear conceited, I would say that I have had a singular upbringing among the sage and sophisticated. There are few others, ever fewer men my age who have visited the places I have seen, befriended those I call friends, learned from the teachers with whom I have studied. Therefore, I say honestly, I find the majority of my peers a trifle dull. That is why I so much more enjoy the company of more distinguished acquaintances such as Lord and Lady Wolverton.

"When I become a wife, it will be to a man whose thoughts and beliefs can marry and live harmoniously with mine," she concluded.

"Your requirements are not easily satisfied," the Count told her, smiling nonetheless.

"Have you been fortunate in marriage?" she asked, turning the conversation in his direction.

"I was ... until last year when I lost my wife. My daughter is grown, with her own family, and I have found my existence too solitary for my liking.

Odd as it may seem, I, too, am not interested by women who are my peers for they are too set in their ways, grow farther away from their youthful ideals with every passing year. They become quite set with missish notions, the solid foundation of a house where I would prefer not to dwell," the Count explained.

Rosanna was dazzled by Lord Waltham's poetic speech and his frank manner. There was no idle flattery in his tone, no game of cat-and-mouse, the childish game she had been forced into from the first with the Baronet.

They spoke on various topics for upwards of an hour and then, Lord Waltham looked into her eyes and said, "I think that, in the main, we are ideally suited one to the other and should probably not hesitate in tying the nuptial knot at once."

It was a remark made in jest, a foolhardy notion, but they both realized that though he teased there was warmth and interest in his eyes. Something told Rosanna that this man she had met only minutes before, was the answer to the quest she had just begun.

"I am well acquainted with the Count and he is old enough to be ... me!" the Earl of Severn stumbled over his words.

"But Grandmother likes him," Rosanna protested.

"Of course Dorothy does—he reminds her of her late husband, Oscar!"

"That is terribly unfair, Father. We had the entire weekend to become well-acquainted with Lord Waltham, and both found him to be a most honorable man, not at all one I should be embarrassed to find at my side."

Lord Shelton turned away from his daughter and looked into the gilt-framed mirror that hung above their marble drawing room fireplace. "What wrath the heavens have sent down upon my head, to find myself not only to be seated at the same dining table as Lady Christina Chatterbox, but to have my daughter linked to a man perhaps old enough to be my father as well," he lamented. "I would get down on my knees to hear you tell me that the Baronet Playmore will not be joining us as well."

"He has not been included," Rosanna said, though her father addressed the heavens still.

"Rosanna, darling, how lovely you look," Lady Simpson said as she entered the drawing room. "The rose petal motif worked into the lace is most becoming in that delicate pink color," she added, "as well as in blue and yellow and lavender." She remembered that the girl had commissioned the same design in each, so taken was her grandchild with its intricate bodice covered in an overlapping pattern of silk rose petals, the modest decolletage in keeping with the puffed sleeves and just the hint of a train making the dress both elegant and easy to maneuver.

"Arthur, won't you compliment your daughter as well?" his mother-in-law asked.

Lord Shelton took his worried face from the mirror and replied, "Rosanna knows that she looks as lovely as ever . . . . Do you realize what she has planned for Lord Waltham?" he asked Lady Simpson, unable to retain his composure any longer.

"Hopefully the same meal she is planning to serve her other guests," the wise lady answered, knowing full well what her son-in-law meant.

"Dorothy, she has a scheme to make the man her husband!" he exclaimed. "Though I realize I have only myself to blame, having been so easily persuaded she would come to no harm at that She-wolf's hunt party *in your company!* If it were not for me, we should not find ourselves in such a fix this evening, forced to provide alimentary fuel for the pack of them!"

Rosanna was prevented from hearing any more of the violent and unprecedented exchange by Alcott's announcement that Lady Chattering was arrived.

"Like a lamb going to the slaughter!" Lord Shelton sighed as his daughter left the drawing room.

Rosanna and her dear friend embraced as though they had not seen each other in weeks when, in fact, they had just had luncheon at the Café Royal the previous day.

"What a lovely fur," Rosanna said, ruffling the luxurious fox trim of Christina's green velvet cloak. "You must feel completely regal in it!"

"I have long waited for the year to be done—I felt hardly a woman these last months," Christina confessed.

"You need not have worn the blacks for the duration. A month would have sufficed," Rosanna assured her.

"No, no, I owed this devotion to dear Egbert's memory," his widow lamented. "He treated me with only kindness during our marriage. I needed to show him this respect . . . . Now, what news did you wish to tell me yesterday, but felt able to do so only *en privé?*"

"It is all about Lady Wolverton's brother, Count Gregory Waltham," Rosanna whispered.

"Oh? What about him?" Christina asked coolly, unimpressed with his first credentials.

"I believe I am going to marry him," her friend confided.

"But you mustn't, Rosanna. It would be a dreadful mistake," her friend warned without hesitation.

"Why do you say that? He is a perfectly—"

"Believe what I tell you. You must trust me."

"Do you know ill of him that has been kept from me?" Rosanna asked.

"No," Christina answered truthfully. "I know him only slightly. I met him just once before this weekend. He seemed a likable man, but old enough to be your father. Marriage to a man of his age will not afford you much happiness."

"Christina, something happened to change your opinion on this subject the night of the Opera—you must tell me what transpired," Rosanna asked in a soft tone. "Did you receive sad news before we arrived at Covent Garden? I cannot imagine what might have caused you to alter an opinion so carefully thought out."

"Well—" Christina began, but was prevented from offering her hostess any explanation by the arrival of some of Rosanna's other guests.

"We will speak on this again," Rosanna promised as she left Lady Chattering to greet them.

Lady Wolverton preceded her husband and her immediate family, who trailed at her heels. All save Lord Waltham, Rosanna noticed, and found it odd that a man who claimed, three days earlier, that he could not wait to feast on her beauty again, would arrive last. But he did bring with him such a glorious bouquet of roses in all hues of pink that Rosanna forgave his tardiness. In fact, she was left quite breathless.

Two tables for eight each were laid out in the

formal dining apartment. Rosanna had paid careful attention to the seating of her guests. She had realized, somewhat embarrassedly, that if she should sit her father and grandmother at the same table, along with Lady and Lord Wolverton and the Count, it would look quite like the old overseeing the young.

Lady Wolverton and her daughter, along with the Viscount Darnley shared their host's table, along with Missie Fortun and her husband, Byron, two of Rosanna's childhood friends whose year-round residence in Edington, in the South, kept them from seeing as much of each other as would have been preferred.

Lord Wolverton and his brother-in-law joined Celeste Beauford and Ashton Heal at the table of Lady Simpson and Rosanna, along with Christina and Mr. Pericles. Rosanna had seen to it that the tables were so close that the guests at one could still see those at the other, a fact which might have led to greater embarrassment had not Rosanna sat back to back with her father, providing a shield for his ofttimes caustic comments.

"It was a triumphant weekend, Lord Shelton, so sorry that you couldn't join us," Irva Wolverton said. "Lord Wolverton bagged the fox, don't you know."

"I thought it was hare," Lord Shelton answered, admitting silently how poor his own pun was.

Rosanna overheard this exchange and took it as a signal to raise her own voice, hoping her father would quiet his.

"Have you completed the infants' sweater you began at the Wolverton's?" Rosanna asked her grandmother.

"I could barely concentrate on my work, what

56

with Mr. Pericles there to keep me company," Lady Simpson answered, turning to the man in question.

"Your grandmother and I had quite an enjoyable time of it while you were off chasing the poor creature," Mr. Pericles said. "I never did ask you for whom you were working so laboriously," he inquired of Lady Dorothy Simpson.

"They are all for my future great grandchild," she answered proudly, as Rosanna's ears burned that Count Waltham was to hear this.

"Did I not tell you all I was with child?" Rosanna asked jokingly. Her father nearly swallowed his fork. "Actually my grandmother has been knitting since I was born, in the hope of seeing the birth of her next generation," Rosanna added.

"It is a lovely thought, Lady Simpson," Lord Waltham said. "A very moving sentiment," he repeated as though he hoped to father that child.

Lord Shelton choked on his wine and leaned back to whisper in his daughter's ear, "Any more of such talk will send me to an early grave."

"Father, be still, I beg of you," Rosanna pleaded. This was the first dinner party she had given for her friends and she wished to make only the best impression. In this company, one did not get a second opportunity.

She was relieved when the cold cresson soup was served, for it put out the fire in everyone's conversation. Rosanna was not set on her defenses until the dessert was presented for she knew that afterwards the ladies would be forced to let the gentlemen savor their brandies amongst themselves. Would her father seek to turn Lord Waltham's ear? she wondered anxiously. Would he antagonize Lord Wolverton whom, Rosanna knew, had had a violent disagreement in Parliament with him last month? As she meant to make Lord Waltham her husband, she thought, her future hung in the balance.

The ladies were in the drawing room discussing the latest rage from Paris—lace pantaloons that hung beneath an overshift, when Rosanna was surprised by Lord Waltham's premature appearance.

"I should benefit from some fresh air," he whispered in his hostess's ear. "Might I impose upon you to show me to the garden?"

Rosanna was more than delighted she told him, and opened the gilt-edged glass doors that led onto the verdant garden tucked away in the heart of the busy city.

"I would not have you think me too bold, but as our acquaintance began on somewhat intimate terms, I feel I must ask you if the disaccord I sense between you and your father is a sudden one or an accepted fact of your life?" the Count asked.

"Accepted and perennial," Rosanna told the silver-haired gentleman. "Father cannot always remember that his daughter has grown into a woman. And although she still resides in his home, she is far from that little girl who depended upon his protection and guidance. I fear it is my own fault for not having married at a younger age," she admitted.

"I must then take my boldness one step further and propose that you let me remedy that situation by making you my wife," Lord Waltham said.

Rosanna surprised her suitor by maintaining the same calm demeanor she had at the outset of their conversation. "I am flattered, Lord Waltham. But I think it is a decision which you have reached with careful thought and planning, not only that you are intrigued with me."

"My dear, it can be no secret that ours would not be a union of passion, but one of mutual interest—you are wanting a husband who will offer you a degree of sorely desired freedom, and I am in need of a woman who will perform wifely duties—maintain my home, entertain my friends and serve as my companion during the last years of my life," he explained.

"There is a logic that is far more beneficial than a hot-tempered discourse of passion which affects so many and leads them into disconsolate marriages," Rosanna agreed.

"You are a rational thinker as well, I see," Lord Waltham told her. "Aware of what you need and want, uninterested in being courted, unlike so many others in your station of life, by meaningless words of endearment and promises that mortal men, first feeling the power of their youth, cannot hope to keep."

"What must we do to further our understanding?" Rosanna asked him anxiously.

"Surely I must take the matter up with your father," Lord Waltham said.

"That is completely unnecessary," Rosanna explained. "As of my twenty-first birthday, I have been mistress of my own affairs and have a direct voice to my man of business. You might have yours arrange a meeting with him. He is Clifford Bates. You are no doubt familiar with him."

"Then we shall meet at the offices of my attorney at our earliest convenience so that we might agree upon the broad negotiations of our contract," Lord Waltham said.

"That seems satisfactory. . . . All that I ask is that, for the moment, we keep this our secret," she requested without any explanation.

"As you wish, Lady Shelton," he said, bringing her hand to his lips.

They returned to the others now reassembled in the drawing room. Rosanna wore a pleasing smile, utterly proud at herself for having completed her self-appointed task with speed. It was difficult for her not to tell her news to her friend, Christina, or to her family, but she knew it was not the appropriate time. She could wait to share her good fortune, she thought to herself as she sipped a glass of champagne and took one of the little iced cakes Alcott proffered.

In the morning, Lady Shelton and her man of business, Clifford Bates, presented themselves at the offices of Reginald, Huxley and Danube, esquires-at-law. Lord Waltham was already seated in the chamber of Sir Montgomery Reginald. He rose to greet his fiancée, tossing aside the notes he had been reading.

Sir Reginald began to read the particulars of his client's offer when they had all taken their seats.

"Lord Waltham has generously agreed to provide his wife with a monthly stipend of three thousand pounds for personal and household requirements. In addition, he has established accounts at the leading women's haberdashers in London. Lady Shelton is to receive, in her own name, the London townhouse and may also choose to reside with the Count at his estate in Northampton. Both homes are already fully staffed; however, if Lady Shelton finds that the servants do not meet her standards, they will be dismissed from Lord Waltham's employ as soon as suitable families can be found for them.

"Lady Shelton will be free to find servants that meet her approval. Any personal servants are invited to live with her at either residence and will be maintained as they are presently. Lady Shelton will also receive, as the Count's wife, her own carriage and groom, her own box at the Opera and at the Royal Theater and membership in any club of her choice.

"In exchange of the above, Lord Waltham requests that Lady Shelton agree to act as his hostess when he wishes to entertain his acquaintances in his home and that she accompany him to any other social commitments he might feel it necessary to make, these limited to three per week and no more than ten in any given month. Lady Shelton is free to pursue any interests she fancies, as long as they do not conflict with the Count's monthly requirements.

"Whether or not Lady Shelton wishes to concieve a child is the lady's choice, but the Count wishes it known he would not be opposed as he wishes to leave a male heir, his daughter having no offspring of her own and presently being past the age of thirty-five. Any other more personal obligations will be discussed between the Count and Lady Shelton between themselves and in privy," the attorney concluded.

Sir Bates turned to his client and waited for her nod of approval before commencing his declaration.

"Lady Shelton will not be dependent on Lord Waltham's kindness in total for she receives a yearly stipend of twenty-five thousand pounds and is the sole benefactress of both her father and her grandmother's wills.

"Lady Shelton agrees to all the points you have brought forward and only wishes to add that, though she retains the right and freedom to choose her own acquaintances and friends, will do so only in consideration of its effect on Lord Waltham as she would never seek to create any disparagement to his good name or her own. As she is free to pursue her own interests and activities, she agrees to confer with her spouse before embarking on any of these, to maintain full harmony in their two lives.

"We agree with the outline you have proposed, in the main, but Lady Shelton reserves the right to argue particulars in privy," Sir Bates concluded.

The two counselors shook hands on their proposals and concluded the meeting. A few days passed before the final document was drawn, its words precisely composed and expertly penned on parchment which explained why Sir Bates did not present himself at the Shelton home until much later in the week. When he did, he begged her signature and wished her to understand fully that this was not an agreement of marriage but merely an understanding of the conditions of that state of life should Lord Waltham and Lady Shelton decide on such a union.

"In other words, dear Rosanna, the marriage can be planned at any time and canceled just prior to your saying your vows under they eyes of the Lord. Your signature does, however, imply a promise that you have given your word," Sir Bates said as he dipped her pen in the inkwell.

Rosanna was excited by the turn her life had taken and was pondering her fate, looking out on Curzon Street, when her father walked into the room.

"Was that not Sir Bates's carriage that departed?" he asked.

"Indeed, Father, it was," she said in a voice more like a song.

"And what was his mission? Do not tell me that I have forgotten that I summoned him for some piece of business," Lord Shelton said.

"No, Father, he was here at my asking . . . for the signing of my nuptial contract with Lord Waltham," she said, unaware that her father was about to faint dead away.

"I cannot believe my ears, daughter, that you would make such a decision without your father's counsel."

"Father, I have long been of age, and have had my own direct counsel in Sir Bates. I need not your approval," she reminded him, "only your blessing."

"That, I am not presently free to give you," he told her.

"So be it," she said. "I will not stand here waiting for it." And she drew up her bonnet from the sofa table, tied it quickly under her chin and quit the house, walking on foot towards South Molton Street and her favorite lace shop.

Rosanna was not about to let her father spoil her high spirits with his doubts on the match. She would begin shopping for her trousseau, she thought. What a joyous endeavor that would be, selecting all that finery of satin and silk done with velvets and lace.

The late May morning was crisp and fresh. The thin gilet Rosanna had tossed over her shoulders kept her warm until she reached the tree-lined street where she most favored browsing and buying. From Le Boudoir, she selected a half-dozen white night shifts, each embroidered with a different Brussels lace, two of which had matching robes that flowed into a long train and had voluminous puffed sleeves and a satin ribbon closure at the neck. She chose ladies' apparel in soft pinks and mauves, a daffodil yellow and a cream, a champagne, an ivory—camisoles and pantelettes and petticoats, handsewn garments worked with the most intricate stitchery and fine detail. Many of the styles had to be commissioned by special order, but there were things Rosanna was able to purchase at once—matching sachets in hearts and rounds, filled with potpourris of exotic herbs and essences, boudoir pillows trimmed with ribbons, embroidered with hearts and doves and butterflies. The shopkeeper suggested she send her groom around to fetch home the packages, but Rosanna was filled with such enthusiasm that she wished to carry them home at once. She had lingered so long in the shop that she did not realize that the weather had changed from that of a sunny day to one of beclouded skies. As she bustled into the street, it appeared as though the heavens would open to shower her with its largest drops of moisture.

In her hurry to catch a hackney coach on the other side of the lane, she ran smack into a tall figure of a gentleman walking towards her.

"Confound it!" she cried as she disentangled herself from the man and caught sight of another lady, one more fortunate, climbing inside the carriage.

"I should think a pardon-me would be more appropriate," the handsome gentleman said as he gazed down at Rosanna. "But, lest you think me the worst brute, allow me to help you gather your parcels. You have dropped a few." He knelt swiftly to collect them before their paper wrappings became soaked on the wet pavement.

"You are very kind," Rosanna said. "A thousand pardon-me's. How can I thank you for your thoughtfulness? My packages contain goods of fabrics so delicate only a moment in the rain would ruin them."

"I am afraid your worst fears will be confirmed

if we do not take shelter at once—there does not appear to be another hackney in sight. Might I suggest the Silver Billet," he said, indicating the pretty silver and black awning just a few steps away.

"A most wonderful idea," Rosanna answered as she let the terribly gallant blond-haired man whose name she did not even know, escort her inside an establishment she had frequented only once before.

Chapter Five

They were quickly seated at a window table in the cozy teahouse, Rosanna unable to tear her gaze away from her handsome companion's laughing, green eyes. His blond hair had been tousled across his forehead by the rain and wind and now made him look all the more attractive. Angelic, Rosanna thought, with a healthy dose of the devil at the same time.

He wore a suit with a pinstripe that made him look very much the man of business, but Rosanna was sure by his air of nobility that he must be a man of title, if not already, one due to inherit shortly.

His broad cheeks gave way to a large smile as he watched Rosanna lift the soggy bonnet from her head and shake her black curls.

"I must look a fright," she said self-consciously.

"You are at present a most romantic vision," he

insisted and extended his hand. "I am Sir Charles Cavanaugh."

Rosanna was about to offer her hand when she suddenly drew back, realizing the impropriety of introducing herself to a stranger in so public a place. His charming manner was making her lose all her good senses, she realized. How could she have even accepted his invitation to tea! she questioned herself severely, but knew the answer without even having to think upon it. She was entranced by his handsomeness and his sophisticated demeanor. *And I would not have my pretty trousseau ruined*, she added to the list as the only rational reason for her actions. But she knew that had played little enough part in it.

"No, I think that I shall not tell you my name just yet," she toyed with him.

"Then I must give you one," he said. "Perhaps the name of a flower would do well, for your face is as fragile as one and the rain has touched you with its dew. How to choose from all the flora . . . but I have it. You are the rose. Yes." he told her, yet he did not appear to notice her surprise at the uncanniness of his having chosen so accurately, "Lady Rose it shall be, a woman with many adventures—or petals. No other flower has as many petals, except perhaps the mum, but that should not suit you at all for it is brittle and rough and you are delicate and soft. Will you tell me about your other petals?" he asked. "Your other adventures?"

Rosanna was at first too startled by his words to speak. Had she not just compared her life to the very same flower, her intrigues and plans to its petals?! How could he have known? She did not doubt he would mind picking off her petals one by one until he reached her heart, such was the look of

67

interest in his eyes. Perhaps she would not mind sharing a few of her petals with him.

"Lady Rose, are men often in the habit of saving you from a thunderstorm?" he persisted, hoping to engage her in conversation.

"Fortunately not. It is only today that I left my house on foot, that I am without my groom and carriage," she answered.

"Then I am to consider myself among the most fortunate of men—perhaps the heavens conspired to have us meet," was his romantic suggestion.

"I think it was my father if anyone for he and I were in the midst of—" Rosanna stopped herself again. She could not, she reminded herself, continue to speak so openly and freely with Sir Cavanaugh, a man she knew not. And she redressed herself anew. "My father thought a walk might improve my complexion," she divined on the spot.

"Your complexion is perfection itself," he said, making it seem not so much flattery as a fact of which she should be proud. "Pray tell me, do you always rely on a rainshower for such radiance?"

Rosanna covered her mouth with her long slender hand to stifle a laugh.

"So you find me amusing?" he asked, pleased just the same. "Then I will ask Lady Rose another question," he continued though Rosanna laughed again upon hearing this strange appellation. "Have you frequented this teahouse often? I ask because I do not believe it suits you in the least. You would appear to find the Café Royal more to your liking," he said, surprising her once again with his intuitiveness.

"You are not mistaken," she answered and wondered if this was a game he was playing, or if he

68

really knew her identity. But, she reasoned, that would mean he was well-connected himself, and able to meet her again under the proper circumstances and that put her at ease. "This is the second time I have rested here though I shop often on this street."

"I, too, have been here only once before, a sorely needed respite after a strenuous shopping excursion," he explained.

"Do you often shop on South Molton Street?" Rosanna asked, knowing that the majority of the shops were for women and house furnishings, affording little enough amusement to a man ... unless his wife brought him along. *Why should that possibility annoy me? It should certainly make me feel less like fresh prey ... But it did not.*

"The circumstances of that other visit were not nearly as pleasurable," Sir Cavanaugh told her. "My companion was not as beautiful as you."

How mysterious. Would he speak of a wife that way? she wondered, intrigued by his green eyes and the way they followed her every move even as she looked about the room as though he were deliberately trying to cast a spell on her. *Such a romantic notion, Rosanna,* she chastised herself, *for one about to wed another.* It was the first time she had thought about Lord Waltham since she met Charles Cavanaugh, and she was not pleased that her intended had intruded on her thoughts.

"Perhaps if I were to think of more amusing topics of conversation, you would be less reticent," Charles Cavanaugh proposed. "Do you travel extensively?"

"Extensively," she echoed, content to merely return his gaze. "My father has taken me abroad with him on numerous occasions. France, Scotland, Denmark, Switzerland."

"I adore France," Charles told her. "At times I even prefer Paris to London," he said, hoping to ascertain her opinion of that subject.

"I am greatly fond of Paris, a city of mystery and intrigue," Rosanna said.

"Yes, I suspect that Lady Rose would adore the Parisian men tagging along on her heels," he teased her.

"Do you believe so?" Rosanna asked him.

"I believe that you most likely have a husband here in London who worries after you caught in the rain," Sir Cavanaugh said, searching for an important answer.

"I do not," Rosanna told him.

"How can that be?" he asked boldly.

"A suitor has never captured my attention for a long enough time to propose," Rosanna answered frankly, but was not willing to admit to him that she had other plans. "I suppose I have not been overly encouraging, being exceedingly fond of my independence. I would need an understanding husband in order to give it up."

"I wonder that there is a man understanding enough to accept a wife who lets herself be caught without groom or carriage by a stranger in the streets of London," he said. "A stranger so obviously interested in making her acquaintance."

"There you have it, a dilemma not easily resolved. I thrive on the spontaneity of our chance meeting and would not exchange it for the tedium of married life without a well-reasoned agreement," she explained. "To have had to relinquish this offer to tea, to offer a hasty beg-pardon and walk the other way—well, it would not do in the least," she said, returning his frankness. "Nor to have to walk to my doorstep in the rain when I can sit here until it ceases."

"I hope that home is not too far from here," he pursued, hoping to learn more about Lady Rose, but that information was not forthcoming.

"Not too far," she answered, a smile on her lips.

"Is it possible to think that I might escort you home?" he asked as they finished their tea and scones.

"Impossible," she said with a smile. "Most inappropriate."

"Are you saying, Lady Rose, that as soon as the heavens close their gates I am forced to lose you forever?"

"That depends on how clever you are, whether you can succeed in finding out who I am and securing a proper introduction," she said, giving him hope.

She parted the curtains of the window and looked outside.

"I've not long before I am to begin the search," he said at the sight of the clearing sky.

"And I must gather up my parcels and return home before my father worries too dreadfully after me," Rosanna told him.

Charles Cavanaugh's interest in Rosanna was so strong that he would not allow her to escape without catching hold of her hand and drawing it to his lips. "Until we meet again, Lady Rose," he said and stood to watch her leave. He was not unaware that all other heads turned to follow her as well.

"You look a fright, granddaughter," Lady Simpson said without so much as lifting her head from the afghan she was crocheting.

"How can you tell, Grandmother?" Rosanna asked.

"You were caught in the rain without so much as a parasol—it did not look like inclement weather when you quit us," the lady said. "You should have asked me to accompany you. I should have been grateful for the fresh air, and my presence would have assured the groom and carriage at our disposal. I am not so headstrong as you," Lady Simpson said by way of reprimand.

"Where is Father?" Rosanna asked, desirous of a change in subject.

"He prepares for a visit from your Lord Waltham. His servant sent round a note, requesting an audience," her grandmother informed her.

"For what purpose I wonder," Rosanna said.

"To plan the wedding, of course. You cannot doubt that is the next logical step in your scheme."

"I suppose not," Rosanna said, though she had not thought Lord Waltham would act upon their arrangement so quickly.

"What do you have in those packages?" her grandmother asked as she heard the paper wrappings rustle as Rosanna turned to leave the room.

"The beginnings of my trousseau," Rosanna said with a contrived look of excitement on her face. She was forcing herself into the role of the blushing bride, but she knew it was not in her heart. Yes, she had enjoyed her shopping excursion, but had not in her heart the express aim of pleasing her future husband. She wondered if her grandmother believed in her high spirits or saw through the pretense.

When her father descended promptly, Rosanna wasted little time in asking after Charles Cavanaugh.

Her first question received little more than a shocked expression.

"Do you know him, Father?" she was forced to ask again.

"Indeed I do, he is the son of the Earl of Clifford, James Cavanaugh, a most notable peer and an old friend of mine as well. I daresay you met the Earl and his son when you were much the babe, but their family circumstances—not unlike ours," he said, referring to his lovely Lila's death, "kept us from being more socially inclined. And to tell you true, I had no idea that his son, Sir Charles, was returned from Ireland, his birthplace. A powerful and influential clan, Rosanna. But now that I have satisfied your curiosity, you must tell me from where it stems," he asked.

If Rosanna had taken an interest in young Cavanaugh, perhaps there might be a way to further it—and have Charles supercede Lord Waltham at the altar to boot, thought the Earl. If only he had learned of Sir Cavanaugh's return to England sooner, the entire melee with the irascible Count might have been avoided!

"His name was mentioned to me today as someone I should know, but I had never heard mention of it before," Rosanna said, certain that any elaboration of their meeting would incur her father's wrath and that she was not wont to do twice in one day. She knew that she must maintain the correct composure for Lord Waltham's visit, all too soon upon them.

The Count's recent intimacy with Rosanna led

him to kiss her full on the cheek when he greeted her. She was not overly pleased with his taking this liberty and it took all her strength to keep from pulling away sharply when he first approached her. She was forced to wonder what he would expect from her after the wedding, whether he would be agreeable to their having separate bedchambers, separate lives . . . .

"Lady Simpson, Rosanna, Lord Shelton, I am pleased that we can begin preparing for the very special events that will unite our two families. I am certain that we are all agreed this should be well-celebrated, Rosanna's first marriage. I have been toying with a few dates, but should like to know which appeals to the bride," the groom-to-be said without any hesitation.

To say that Rosanna was taken aback with this deluge of wedding details would be insufficient. She was unprepared to make these decisions, not the least bit anxious to discuss them, and a bit terrified at the thought of actually taking those steps that woul lead her to be Lord Waltham's wife.

"We are already in the last week of April," Rosanna began after some pause. "I should think we would need until the first of June." Could she stall for more time, she wondered and was about to ask it of her—could it be?—fiancé, when he pounced (as best a man his age could).

"The first of June is a delightful day. A capital suggestion," Lord Waltham said with vigor. "By all means, it shall be the first of June." He seized his intended's hand and kissed it at once.

"The first is a very lovely day," Lady Simpson concurred.

"Then I may consider it concluded," Lord Waltham said, moving a bit too fast for Rosanna's

74

taste. Yet she nodded her approval. Why prolong these last few weeks of unmarried life, she reasoned with herself, when it was the advantages of the other state that most concerned her.

"My daughter Lucy has volunteered to assist me in the composition of my guest list," Lord Waltham continued.

"Your daughter?" Lord Shelton echoed, unaware until now of her existence.

"Yes, she will be coming to London from her home in Somersetshire for the weekend next," he explained.

"She is grown then," Lord Shelton inferred.

"Indeed, a woman of thirty-seven," Lord Waltham beamed proudly.

"A nice older sister for Rosanna," her father said, sarcastically.

"Yes, and she will be entirely at your disposal for the posting of the invitations and any other business involved in the planning of the wedding," Lord Waltham added, patting Rosanna's hand gently. "Now, shall we have an evening wedding or a morning affair?" he asked, unaware of her indifference.

"As you wish, Gregory," Rosanna insisted, trying to accustom herself to his name. Whatever way could conclude the ceremony with as little pomp would be her choice.

"A morning ceremony with a nuptial breakfast," the fiancé proposed.

"Yes, that would be perfectly charming," Rosanna said, trying to muster a little enthusiasm.

"With only five weeks before us, we shall have to begin on your gown at once," Lady Simpson said, hoping to brighten the expression on her granddaughter's face, trusting no one save herself had noticed. The dear lady wondered if she should broach the subject of her downtrodden appearance with the girl, but thought it only jitters that did cause her mind to wander and her spirits to dampen.

"I am surprised at all the fuss you make," Lord Shelton spoke his piece. "I should think that on the occasion of your second marriage, you would wish less of a to-do."

"It is only that I think of your daughter's happiness, that her wedding must be all the wondrous things which a young girl dreams," Lord Waltham explained.

"That is very kind and dear of you," Rosanna said, on her betrothed's behalf. He was as ever the thoughtful and tender man she had first met and she began to feel remiss because of her lack of interest. What had happened to so quickly and completely change her composure? Was it the feeling of inevitability? The close proximity of the first of June? The feeling of entanglement? Or was it meeting Sir Charles Cavanaugh?

Rosanna tried to banish the thought of the handsome stranger, but was finding it increasingly difficult to do . . .

"You are more than kind," Lord Waltham answered her.

"No more than you," Rosanna said, taking his hand now. If he wished this to be a *cause celebre*, she forced herself to think, was it not her duty to see that he was made happy? Was that not, after all, the task she had undertaken by agreeing to exchange marriage vows? "Will you be joining us for dinner?" she asked as she realized the hour grew late.

"I am afraid that I cannot. There are many

76

preparations I must make for my daughter's arrival," Lord Waltham explained.

"You will have to bring her here for a small dinner party when she arrives," Lady Simpson insisted. "We are all anxious to make your family ours," she added graciously.

For her part, Rosanna shared her father's relief at Lord Waltham's departure. She did not think that she could muster the energy needed to sustain polite dinner conversation amongst the four of them; she certainly had no desire to expound on wedding plans. She instructed Alcott to send dinner to her room where she would be resting.

"What? No theater party nor soiree tonight?" her father asked, surprised yet relieved. "Perhaps Lord Waltham's effect on you will be for the better," he said, though not believing it.

"It has been quite a harrowing day," Rosanna explained. "I am sorely in need of the quietude of my own apartment."

"Go on with you, Rosanna," Lady Simpson said. "Do not pay your father any mind. He has you at home for once and is still not pleased."

Rosanna kissed her gratefully, kissed her father dutifully, and went to her chamber where Betty assisted in the removal of her well-worn clothes. She slipped into a familiar nightshift, though night had hardly fallen. She sank appreciatively into the soft mattress of her bed and rested her head on the satin pillow. She thought of her upcoming wedding, but saw, in her mind's eye, not a picture of Count Gregory Waltham, but one of Sir Charles Cavanaugh.

How can I think of him? she asked herself, well aware of the answer. Something in his manner intrigued her. The laughter in his eyes interested her, his poised, debonair demeanor touched the very center of her heart. She hoped that he was as enterprising a gentleman as he appeared; though she was cross with herself for thinking it, she looked forward to seeing him again.

Chapter Six

Lord Shelton sat within a drawing room all too familiar to him, though he had not found himself within its confines in some time. He had not been looking forward to returning to this place he knew so well, but this visit was imperative. He had spent many an evening in front of this fireplace, sipping a brandy with his admired friend, now departed. Memories filled his mind as he stood with his arm leaning on the mantlepiece, supporting his corps, not a little unnerved at the impending meeting with his friend's widow, Lady Christina Chattering.

"I have not welcomed you here in some time," Christina said as she entered the room. "How do you do?"

"I am well, Lady Chattering," he said with great formality. "You are looking quite well," he felt compelled to add.

"I am sorry I kept you waiting for so long, but your visit is, shall we say, surprising?"

"Lady Chattering," he began, walking towards the divan she sat upon, "I am here to bury any feelings of ill will . . . for my daughter's sake."

"But I have no ill feelings towards you, Lord Shelton. I was gracious to you from the first. My husband introduced you as among his immediate circle and I welcomed you into our home as I do now. It was when I became confidant to your daughter that you snubbed me," Christina said, never understanding why her friend's father had taken such a cool dislike to her.

His steel-like eyes looked away from her now.

"I realize that it would be easier if I ignored what has transpired between us . . . this conversation would proceed more easily, but I wish to understand why you have behaved in so humiliating a fashion," she continued.

"Perhaps it was that I was envious of my friend . . ."

"Do not flatter me, Lord Shelton. Simply tell me what is in your heart, and what brings you here today," she said, aware that whatever it was, he was not prepared to greatly alter his opinion of her.

"It is my daughter. I have come to beg of you a most precious favor. It is not for me—I have no doubt it is too precious to ask for myself. I ask it for Rosanna whom you have befriended, for whom I pray you wish only happiness."

"Has something terrible befallen Rosanna?" Christina asked as she rose to her feet.

"Nothing like that, dear lady," Lord Shelton allayed her fears and helped her back to her seat. "But she is on the brink of making a most tragic

80

error in judgment, one she will regret the rest of her life."

"What do you mean, Lord Shelton?" her friend asked, her eyebrows knotting with concern.

"I speak of her intended marriage to Lord Waltham. Though I am not certain you would find it as much of a catastrophe as—"

"Her *marriage* to Lord *Waltham?*" Christina could hardly believe her ears. "But when did this come about? She has not mentioned a word of this mischief to me!"

"And I thought it was your example that led her to this," Rosanna's father said, relieved that she shared his concern, hopeful for the first time that day that he might have an ally, a powerful one. "I am pleased with your reluctance to embrace this news, but I did not think it a mistake to assume you led her to believe this idea of hers might suit the lifestyle she wishes to lead."

"I must confess that at first I did, but by a peculiar succession of events I was reminded of something that happened to me a number of years ago. I realized that while the circumstances of four years ago enabled me to marry Lord Chattering with an open heart, Rosanna is not in that same situation. I have spent the past few days discouraging her from pursuing Lord Waltham. I suppose that her knowledge of my disapproval has led her to keep this news from me. I had little idea that she was proceeding twice as rapidly as she let on," Christina said, feeling somewhat betrayed. "But I have done all I thought I could to dissuade her. What do you ask of me now?"

"I would like you to give a dinner party, at my expense naturally, in a few days," Lord Shelton said.

"I should think your cook can prepare a meal as well as mine," Christina said, but the humor was lost to the Earl.

"There is more . . . there is a young man I wish very much to be here. Sir Charles Cavanaugh."

"Can you not invite him to your own party?" Christina asked, now genuinely confused.

"No, because then Rosanna would see right through my scheme. As it is now, we plot with great risk," he warned her.

"Lord Shelton, a moment's breath, I beseech you. Until today you have not so much as accepted one of my invitations, and now I find you wish me to throw a small bash with a guest list of your own making?" Christina asked.

"For Rosanna," Lord Shelton repeated. "Rosanna."

"But how does Rosanna enter into this? And who is Charles Cavanaugh?"

Lord Shelton unraveled the mystery of Sir Cavanaugh, reminding her of her husband's acquaintance, Lord James Cavanaugh, and elaborated on his daughter's story enough to say he suspected she had more than heard the gentleman's name, had perhaps met the man himself, a suspicion formed largely on Christina's not knowing of him. "For who has introduced Rosanna to all the acquaintances she fancies now but you, dear lady," he said.

"And so you propose this dinner party to formally introduce them in the hopes that Rosanna will end her alliance with the Count?" Christina asked, solving the puzzle.

"Precisely," her guest affirmed. "The plan came to mind as soon as I ascertained that the future Earl had resumed his residence in London. It would be the perfect match for Rosanna!"

"Lord Shelton, this scheme—though I find it delightful—is fraught with holes. Certain people will have to be invited, and it is exactly their presence you wish to avoid—but if I do not include Lord Waltham and Lady Wolverton and her circle, Rosanna will completely suspect a plot. We must further disguise Sir Cavanaugh's presence here, perhaps with the addition to the list of his father and one or two other of my late husband's intimates . . . . Does this meet with your approval?" she asked, raising an eyebrow. With the extraction of this favor, she doubted the Earl would ever have a negative word to say to her again.

"Indeed, Christina, it is perfect," he said with honest warmth. "I can see that you are a true friend to my daughter. Spare no effort to insure this soiree's success and please direct all accounts receivable to my man of business," he admonished. "It is the least I can do in return."

"You are correct, Lord Shelton, it would be the least and I'll have none of it—I wish a promise of my own. This dinner I do in secret for Rosanna and Rosanna alone—and the surest way for her to find out about your intervention would be through your man of business. Financial assistance is not what I would like from you. Something far more precious and dear, your approval of my friendship with Rosanna—if the truth be spoken, your dislike of me has in part led your daughter down this hasty path to marriage," Christina said, seizing the opportunity to bury their differences at long last.

"You are right, my dear," he said, taking her hand. "You have both my apologies for my unfair treatment and a pledge to serve you as a friend. An old man often thinks himself wise beyond his years, but often forgets he does not see as clearly as he once did," he said and withdrew to let Lady Chattering continue with the details.

I must hurry with the invitations, she thought to herself, *lest I incur my newly won friend's displeasure*. She laughed inwardly.

The Earl could have hardly suspected just how in his favor events were turning. For as he approached his parliamentary chambers that afternoon, his daughter was being called upon by none other than Sir Cavanaugh, more enterprising than Rosanna had dared hope.

Charles Cavanaugh had wasted little enough time solving the riddle of his Lady Rose. It had happened easily enough at his men's club, Peppernell's, where he had been discussing the various merits of certain female acquaintances of his friend, Mr. Robert Daniels.

Sir Cavanaugh began to recount the recent episode on South Molton Street and succeeded in arousing the interest of certain young men in their immediate circle. One head, belonging to Lord Peter Wrent, looked round from a winged-back armchair whose stuffing was in bad need of repair; another looked up from a morning daily—Sir Ivan Bowles, the club's champion billiardist.

"Her skin was of the finest alabaster, her hair black as midnight, her eyes, stars in the dark heavens," Charles was saying. "Her lips like two rubies, and her cheeks ablush with rose—tis why I did dub her Lady Rose, for she had both the softness and delicacy of the flower as well as a character as complex as the configuration of its petals."

"If the lady would hear you go on this way," Sir Ivan jested, "she'd have you at the altar before you saw midnight again!"

"If she has half the attributes Sir Charles assigns her," Robert Daniels interjected, "she may have me at the church this noon." And here he feigned a female swoon.

"Taunt me as you will," Charles Cavanaugh began his defense, "you'll envy me on the morrow."

"Your Lady Rose does fit the description of one London lovely that comes to mind," Lord Wrent said, "And if she is your Lady Rose, your choice in appellation is divine inspiration."

"Whom do you suspect, my lord?" Bob Daniels egged him on.

"Let us look at the facts," Lord Wrent went on. "The lady must be of the noblest birth—any other would have gladly offered her name to one who appeared in such Jermyn Street finery," the lord could not deny himself the playful dig.

"Come now, Lord Peter," Sir Ivan reprimanded him with a slap on the back. "Soon you'll have our newest recruit blushing like a maid."

"Now, now, Sir Charles has been back from the wilds of Eire for two months—we've no longer to handle him with our gloves on!" Lord Wrent insisted. "So, the young gallant has given us a description of a fair complexion, not singular among our beauties—"

"And all too few of these are there," Mr. Daniels chirped.

"Indeed, but back to the specifics, a long mane of raven hair, and that you unwittingly dubbed her the Lady Rose—is it not obvious?" Lord Wrent asked his cronies.

"You'll string me up too far now, Peter Wrent. Give me her name or I'll have your Whig neck." Sir Charles insisted, though his broad grin was ever upon his lips.

"'Tis plain to me, if Lord Peter won't tell," Sir Ivan Bowles said. "It can be none other than Lady Rosanna Shelton, daughter of the Earl of Severn."

"Rosanna?" Sir Charles echoed in disbelief. "But our fathers are well-acquainted. 'Tis the work of fate!"

"Good grief, Bonnie Charlie!" his friend, Mr. Daniels, exclaimed. "You shall have your hands full with that vixen!"

"Whatever do you mean?" Sir Charles asked, well used to his friends' favored nickname.

"Only that she has made it her business to snub every suitor who has dared cross her path since her come-out," his friend elucidated. "Prefers quite a wild set—Lady Wolverton et al."

"But how could you not yet be aware of Lady Shelton?" Lord Wrent asked. "You cannot be long in London without hearing her name mentioned or catching a glimpse of the lovely at the Opera."

"I've not been in London all that long, Lord Wrent, nor do I spent my time in idle revery of all her beauties . . . unlike certain gentleman with whom I am acquainted," he said, not resisting this opportunity to chastise their endless theorizing on the subject.

"We do not know *all* her beauties," Robert Daniels responded, intimating, however, that they knew quite a few. "But what is imperative at this moment is that you make Rosanna Shelton's acquaintance before she forgets the petal she dropped in South Molton Street."

"She is not entirely accessible," Sir Cavanaugh was sure.

"Then you will leave your card at the Curzon Street residence and call again on the morrow," Lord Wrent, a self-confessed expert in these dealings, suggested. "But beware of her Grandmama!"

Charles Cavanaugh was a bit too impatient for that scheme, he thought later that day, and decided to spend the late morning hours observing the Shelton household until such time as any figure resembling a butler exited, feeling confident that he could talk his way past any chamber maid or pantry assistant. He did not count on Lady Dorothy Simpson greeting him at the front door when he boldly knocked, though forewarned he was.

"Goodness, I thought you the haberdasher's boy," Lady Simpson exclaimed upon the sight of Sir Cavanaugh's calling card. "I must ask your forgiveness and your silence in not repeating this to my son-in-law. Perhaps you will tell me what I can do for you, Sir Charles Cavanaugh," she asked, reading from his card.

"I have come hoping to see your granddaughter. I believe we met the other day in South Molton Street—I have been anxious after her health as we were both caught in a horrendous downpour . . ." he stopped, convinced that the lady was not listening to a word he said.

Indeed, he was correct. Lady Simpson was busy trying to place the young man's handsome face. "Are you not the son of James Cavanaugh, the Earl of Clifford?" she asked, uncertain of her memory.

"Yes, dear lady, I am," he confessed.

"But you have not been in London in some time—why it has been years since I have seen your father . . ." she mused as she kept the young man standing precariously on the landing of the house. "Oh, but this is very rude of me, Sir Charles, do come in." She ushered him into the drawing room.

"As you can see," Lady Simpson went on with

her apology, "our butler is out-of-doors. You must amuse yourself while I see if Rosanna is home to visitors."

"I would be most grateful, Lady Simpson," he said, aware that Rosanna might not wish to trouble herself upon such short notice; that Rosanna might not be his Lady Rose did not seem a possibility any longer.

It did not take Rosanna's appearance for Sir Cavanaugh to know he was in the right home. All it required was a look around the drawing room to the portrait that hung above the fireplace mantle. It was a portrait in oils of Lady Rose—Rosanna, he corrected himself. He judged the work to be no more than four years old, done about the time of her come-out.

He thought her even more beautiful the other day, her hair mussed by the rain, her composure slightly dampened by the weather. He would have been surprised to learn that on this fair day she found herself more discomfited than ever as her grandmother told her who awaited her below.

"Charles Cavanaugh is here? Now?" she asked, ready to tear out her magnificent hair with her hands. "How has he done it?"

"By coach, I suspect," Lady Simpson offered, misunderstanding her granddaughter's surprise.

"What am I to do?" Rosanna asked. "What shall I wear? What has happened to Betty—I'll need her to coif this hair!"

"Rosanna, you must regain your senses—this is hardly the behavior befitting a young lady who is to be married in a month," Lady Simpson warned and suddenly put all the pieces of her granddaughter's puzzle together: Rosanna's lethargy, her indifference towards the wedding plans, her animated excitement at Sir Cavanaugh's appearance. "What are we to do indeed?" she asked.

"Grandmama, you must descend and keep him company until I am ready," she said as she sat at her boudoir table and began to pinch her cheeks ferociously.

"Rosanna, perhaps you had better tell me how you made Sir Cavanaugh's acquaintance?" her grandmother asked.

"He helped me to a hackney in the rainstorm when I was shopping the other day," Rosanna said, leaving out a good part of the adventure, though telling the truth nonetheless. It was not that Rosanna was in the habit of lying; she merely judged, in this instance, that any additional details would be less than warmly received.

"I can see that you are in no condition to explain the truer circumstances of Sir Cavanaugh's visit—how you fret in front of that mirror! I will send Betty to you, with specific instructions that you are not allowed to dawdle here all day. He awaits you, Rosanna!" her grandmother said, wondering how she was going to broach this subject with her son-in-law.

Betty was at her mistress's side just in time to salvage what was left of the curl she had put in Lady Shelton's hair the day before.

"You have done a bit of damage, Miss," Betty said, with nothing like reproach in her voice, more rather an apology for why she would not be able to arrange the twists in as beautious a style as she wished.

"I am fortunate that I did not tear it out at the very roots, so flustered am I by a sudden caller,"

Rosanna said. "I must look as special as you can arrange," she near pleaded with the abigail.

Betty helped Rosanna select a silk gown in a deep mauve shade, with rose buds embroidered at the hem and cuffs in a slightly deeper hue of silk thread.

"Entirely appropriate," Rosanna said aloud, "if he still thinks of me as Lady Rose."

Rosanna was so anxious to see Charles Cavanaugh that she thought she would fly down the stairscase but remembered her demeanor as she approached the foyer landing.

"Here is Rosanna," Lady Simpson called out then, turning to the girl added, "Come and greet Sir Cavanaugh that I may see after some refreshment." As she passed Rosanna on the threshold of the drawing room whispered, "Alcott is not yet returned."

"You look fully recovered from the downpour, a more beautiful vision, if that is possible," Sir Charles said as he walked to her side.

"I am amazed to see you again . . . so soon after our tea," Rosanna said unabashedly.

"It was not difficult to find you—you are one of the most sought after and talked about ladies of London," he admitted.

"And you, Sir Cavanaugh, are one of its most eligible bachelors," she said, "though you are only recently returned to us."

They sat down and Sir Charles proceeded to tell Rosanna of his home in Ireland and of the familial obligations that had kept him there for so long.

"I left London five years ago, when Father thought it best that I learn the workings of our estate."

"I have been abroad many times with my own father, but never to Ireland. Is it very beautiful?" Rosanna asked.

"Indeed, very rich and verdant, very romantic. The oldest families all live in castles surrounded by moats with drawbridges and turrets. There is far more countryside, less industry in the land as I know it. The sunsets are more colorful than anywhere else in the world," he assured her. "I think it a sight you would enjoy."

"I've no doubt," Rosanna said, "particularly with one as able as you for my guide, you must know the most correct vantage point." She showed no inclination to redress her confidential tone, as though Count Gregory Waltham and their impending marriage had completely slipped her mind. She did not desire to be reminded of that just now. Had not Lady Simpson joined them once again, a short time later, there is no telling where there conversation might have led.

If Sir Cavanaugh had suggested their whisking away right now to a vessel awaiting on the western shore to take them to see the sights he described, one could not be certain Rosanna would have voiced the least objection. Lady Simpson's presence forced their discussion to take on a much less excited pitch. And then it seemed all too soon that Sir Cavanaugh had to take his leave without Rosanna's having heard nearly enough about him.

He was all she could think of that afternoon, a fact that disturbed Lady Simpson.

"Have you forgotten completely about Count Waltham?" Lady Dorothy asked.

"Of course not!" Rosanna answered brusquely, aghast at her own transparency.

"Shouldn't we talk about your caller's surprising visit?"

"There is nothing to say—Sir Cavanaugh merely wished to satisfy his own curiosity that I arrived home safely from South Molton Street," Rosanna explained.

"Then why did he not send round a note that very afternoon?" Lady Simpson asked.

"How can I be accountable for his actions?" Rosanna asked, set on edge by the interrogation. She felt only guilt at her interest in young Sir Charles. "I doubt I shall even see him again," she added, though praying for the contrary.

He had not given her any indication that he wished to be any more than an acquaintance, and even if he did, she told herself, that was no reason to think about putting aside her well-thought wedding plans.

"Lord Waltham's daughter will be here on the morrow," Lady Simpson said. "We should begin to compose our guest list so that we might have that to discuss with her." If Rosanna insisted that Sir Cavanaugh was nothing more than a friend, she would not push the matter any further.

"I will fetch paper and pen," Rosanna said and soon found herself marking, at the top of the list, not the name of her friend Christina Chattering nor that of her groom, but *Sir Charles Cavanaugh*. She somehow noticed it before her grandmother could and scratched it out. But she knew that she could not erase him from her mind as easily.

The May night was warm and clear and the path to the front door of Lady Chattering's house was lined with lanterns that made it possible to see the first signs of buds on the rosebushes that bordered the walk. There was no sign, however, to indicate to all who entered that within these portals, such tranquility was nonexistent. Instead transpired scenes of unrelenting calamity.

"It is the perfect time for your father to make his important announcement," Irva Wolverton whispered to her young friend Rosanna.

"I do not agree for we are not in my home and I shall not detract any of the interest from our hostess with so personal an announcement." Rosanna was adamant.

"You are forsaking the perfect moment," her future sister-in-law contended and did not give up the argument, pausing for merely a second or two to kiss upon each cheek, her distant relation, Gaylord Pericles.

When Mr. Pericles turned to give Rosanna a kiss, he whispered in her ear, "Congratulations are offered, dear lady. You have wasted no time in finding a suitable match."

"It is a secret I should not wish to unveil tonight," she answered in a hushed voice, reproving his knowing wink.

Mr. Pericles left these ladies to greet two others, his cousins Alana Quentin and Celeste Beaufort, sipping champagne at the far end of the room without benefit of their suitors' presence, specifically to inquire after their whereabouts.

Lord Waltham took Gaylord's place beside his sister and his future bride and bent nearly to one knee to kiss Rosanna's hand. She worried about the spectacle he was making and begged him to rise.

"You are ever the man in love," his sister told

93

him. "Yet it becomes you—you look a sight younger for it."

Waltham begged his sister's pardon as he swept his fiancé to the divan.

"You are lovely this evening," he said to her. "I will be a most proud husband."

Rosanna bent her head humbly, wishing to escape this tender scene she and the Count were acting out for any who noticed. They had struck a far too intimate pose and she longed to redress herself, so was grateful when her father approached, asking to speak with the Count alone.

Rosanna looked about the room for her hostess whom she had not yet greeted, the butler having ushered each of the guests inside the vast and elegantly appointed drawing room. Rosanna's gaze was caught by a familiar figure entering the room. Sir Charles Cavanaugh.

Sir Charles had been surprised by Lady Chattering's invitation—he had not yet made her acquaintance—but as quickly as he learned of her close friendship with the Shelton family, he accepted the request for the honor of his presence. Rosanna rose to her feet and began walking towards him as though governed by a will other than her own. When she realized what she was doing, he had already noticed her and that broad grin again appeared. He walked the rest of the distance to be at her side. He took her hand in a less flamboyant style than Lord Waltham, which she appreciated, for she would have found it twice as hard to explain any intimacy with Sir Cavanaugh.

"I would like you to meet my father," Charles told her as he led her back towards the foyer.

"Lady Shelton!" the Earl of Clifford exclaimed

94

upon their introduction. "The last time I saw you, you were so high and answering to the name of 'Little Rosie,'" he said, making her blush. "It has been far too long," he told her with his thick Irish accent his son had not inherited. "Is your father here?"

"Yes, by the fireplace," Rosanna said, indicating the path.

"I must speak with him at once," Lord Cavanaugh said, leaving the two young people to themselves.

"Fate brings us together again," Charles said.

"Most thankfully," Rosanna said boldly, her eyes looking deeply into his, an undeniable smile on her lips. Though she tried to hide it from all others, she was sure she was smitten by Charles Cavanaugh and was not entirely sure of what she was going to do about it. She turned away from him for a moment, so that perhaps he would not notice the captivated interest in her eyes.

"Rosanna," he called her name softly to regain her attention. Her eyes turned to look into his as he spoke, "Do you not think our meeting written in the heavens, to find ourselves here as our first acquaintance—as if by chance? It is mysterious work."

"By the heavens or an able hostess, I care not which. Each time I see you, I feel changed in some way, taken out of myself suddenly, and suddenly partaking of yours. You are a man no woman would like to live without meeting," Rosanna confessed, unable to hide her interest, not even wanting to.

"You are an accomplished flirt," he said, venturing forth to see if she merely toyed with him.

"Sir Cavanaugh, that is too unkind—and certainly untrue," she chided him, but without anger.

95

"The persuasive manner with which you spoke of your ancestral home in Ireland, just the other day, left me wishing to hear more."

Rosanna had little idea that these last words flattered him the most and prompted him to a discourse that—were he any other man—would have put his listener into sound slumber. But Charles Cavanaugh could, one was sure, find a provocative way to describe an earthworm, and so entranced Rosanna Shelton that he had her completely in his grasp for upwards of half an hour.

It was only when a curious Gaylord Pericles joined them, to bid them a good evening as he sought a piece of news about this handsome stranger, that Rosanna realized she could not remain in such close confinement with Sir Cavanaugh all evening (much as she would have preferred). Rosanna looked about the room for her friend and hostess, Christina. A shiver ran down her back as she saw, not Lady Chattering, but the Earl of Clifford, engaged in conversation with her father and none other than Lord Gregory Waltham. Her fears quickly multiplied. What if the Count said or did something that would indicate her relationship with him? She would lose Charles Cavanaugh's attention by the morrow. This would not do at all ...

Perhaps her father would keep the news from his friend's ears, she thought, and then wondered what possible reason he could have for doing so. What difference did it make since Sir Cavanaugh would learn the truth sooner or later, she ultimately reasoned. And what could she hope to come of their friendship if he did not? *There, I have spoken the words. Sir Charles and I can never be more than friends.* But something in Rosanna's heart told her that would never do either.

It was unfortunate that Rosanna did not know of her father's meddling for it would have put her mind to rest on the subject of her secret engagement. Lord Shelton was prepared to keep the Earl of Clifford in the dark; for the truth to be known would certainly put a crimp in his plans. He had his eye on his daughter and Sir Charles quite often during their conversation and was pleased that his suspicions about their chance meeting had been confirmed. He had discussed this aim with his mother-in-law that very evening, while Rosanna was still in her dressing gown upstairs, and had arranged for Lady Simpson to divert the Count's attention so that he might speak with Lord Cavanaugh on the subject on their children's future together.

"It is a capital idea, Shelton, and I see that they have taken a fancy to each other... a lovely girl, Rosanna..." the parent said in a hushed voice. "I hope Charles shares my opinion."

Lord Shelton was able to enjoy the rest of the soiree. If only the same could have been said for Lady Simpson who had, moments before, slipped her arm through that of the Count and asked him to accompany her out-of-doors onto the patio.

She was for the first time in twenty-five years in complete agreement with her son-in-law. She could not help but notice Rosanna's complete distraction after Sir Cavanaugh's visit and was in accord with any scheme that kept her from sharing an altar with Lord Waltham. Sharing the evening's breeze alone with him further convinced her. "Boring," she whispered to Arthur Shelton when he gave her the previously arranged signal indicating that his téte-à-éte with James Cavanaugh was complete. She gladly returned to him the task of keeping the Count otherwise engaged from monopolizing Rosanna.

It was still some time before Lady Christina Chattering descended, and when she did she was captured, in a way, by her friend Gaylord Pericles, who pressed her for information. Both were unaware of the presence of the notorious Baronet Playmore who had slipped behind the dining apartment door upon seeing these two, their ears bent one towards the other, a most singular welcome to his tardy arrival.

"How come Rosanna Shelton and Charles Cavanaugh seem to be so *intime*, when I have heard that she is recently engaged to Count Waltham, my own relation?"

"How is it that you have already learned of this when I am not supposed to know?" Christina asked, jealous of his many and varied sources.

"And yet you do know?" he continued, neither one of them having yet answered a question.

"Gaylord, it is too complex a situation to unravel for you now," Christina said.

"I must have some of the facts or I will not behave myself at all this evening," he threatened in a voice she knew well.

"Very well—then I will tell you that her father and I conspire to bring her and Sir Cavanaugh together. We both find your cousin—begging your pardon, dear beloved friend—an abominable mismatch for a girl of her experience," Christina confessed, somewhat ashamedly.

"I find it hard to believe that you and the Earl could agree on anything," he said, letting her know what in her story amazed him the most. "Christina, tell me, what has led you to this sudden change of heart—*Il Barbiere*, perhaps?"

"Gaylord, you know my history too well. I beg you to keep my confidences to yourself, for I intended your ears alone to hear them. Now pray, I must join my guests. The party has gone on too long without me."

Indeed, thought the Baronet Playmore, who wondered which of the guests, though knowing far less which of the secrets he now held, would provide even more fascinating entertainment than the scene he had just overheard.

Chapter Seven

No one was more joyous than the Baronet when it became known that Lady Chattering had orchestrated a buffet on her patio rather than a stuffy seated dinner for, he was certain, left at the mercy of placecards, he would not have been half as close to Rosanna Shelton as he desired. Now he was able to engage her at will.

Rosanna was the only one not pleased with the arrangement as she knew she could not keep pivoting between Lord Waltham and Sir Cavanaugh. She did not know how her parent and grandparent had kept her intended in close conversation, but it was not a feat she could rely upon for the duration. She did not anticipate that her talk with Sir Cavanaugh would be interrupted by another quarter entirely— the Baronet. Since the mishap at the Wolverton estate, he had kept his distance, disavowing any acquaintance with her, much less treading on the brief intimacy of that occasion. But now the Baronet seemed more secure, anxious to renew a dialogue.

"I understand you have some interesting news to share," he said as he approached Rosanna.

Her heart stopped she was sure, while she searched for an answer that would appease him and offer Charles little enough insight. Surely he could not be referring to her engagement, she reasoned, but would not take that chance by asking to what he referred.

"I do not have any news at all," she feigned ignorance. "There is no new luster in my life. But I am certain in the coming months our whole city will take on a warmer glow and there will be more soirees and parties than we can hope to attend."

Lord Playmore shot her a glance that said he knew that was not the answer he had come to seek from her lips, but he would be content to play along with her for a time. He turned the subject round to his own, uninteresting, she thought, pursuits and then suddenly withdrew to seek his hostess. He left Rosanna with a most uneasy feeling that would, in short order, cause her to return, somewhat prematurely to her own home. She was, for the time, grateful that Sir Charles and the Baronet were the vaguest of acquaintances, acknowledging each other with no more than a perfunctory nod, but she knew as well that the Baronet was not one to stand on ceremony when he wished to take action—she had learned that at Lady Wolverton's and worried anew about her secret and the possibility of being undone.

"I think I am in need of some refreshment," Rosanna told Charles. "Shall we adjourn to the patio?"

But as soon as they crossed the room, Rosanna realized she would soon be face to face with Lord Waltham.

"Rosanna," the Count began intimately as he caught sight of her, "I have not seen you all evening. Pray join your father and I," he asked, making no mention of Sir Cavanaugh in the invitation.

Rosanna, always in control, now stood frozen on the spot, not knowing what course of action to take. Finally she spoke, "Sir Cavanaugh was escorting me to the buffet."

"I will see to that," Lord Waltham said, jealousy appearing in his eyes.

"That is not necessary," Rosanna stumbled. "I have suddenly . . . lost my appetite. Actually, I have developed a most ghastly headache and thought some nourishment might dissipate it, but now I am convinced the only remedy is to return home. Father, might we call for our carriage?"

When the Shelton family was assembled in the foyer, with Lady Simpson making their apologies to their hostess, Rosanna turned to look into the room. She was relieved to see Lord Waltham newly engaged in dialogue with his sister. Her vision was next captured by Sir Cavanaugh standing alone just where she had left him. He offered her a smile as their adieu, one she readily returned.

"You have made a conquest," Lady Simpson said, aware of the gentleman as well. "He is smitten with you, Rosanna," she assured her grandchild as they quit Lady Chattering's. "And if I am not mistaken, you are smitten as well."

"That is nonsense," Rosanna said, fighting to banish his portrait from her mind. "I am betrothed to Lord Waltham. There can be no place for Charles

Cavanaugh in my life," she insisted a bit too vehemently.

Lady Simpson needed no more proof than this, but her suspicions were doubly confirmed when Rosanna refused some warm tea to soothe her headache.

"It is gone," she assured her parent and grandparent as they arrived home. "But I will sleep now nonetheless . . . a tiring day it has been."

Lord Shelton was anxious to speak with his mother-in-law, but waited until he heard Rosanna's chamber door close.

"What happened to precipitate that hasty departure?" he asked.

"Rosanna's realization that she is interested in Sir Cavanaugh. I do not think she knew how to dally between him and Lord Waltham at Christina's. And, too, I think, that the Baronet Playmore had a hand in it—Rosanna was not the same after they spoke, I could see that from clear across the room!" Lady Simpson attested, surprising the son-in-law with her quickly drawn conclusions. "But tell me, how successful were you with Lord Cavanaugh?"

"I believe him to endorse our matchmaking with an open heart," the meddlesome father said.

"I hope poor Lord Waltham did not get the gist of our scheme."

"I hope he did!" Lord Shelton assured her. "I should like him to know that I do not approve of him in the least."

"I thought we had agreed to seem as though we do approve, Arthur. You know your daughter! She is a headstrong one, who would not wait to bat an eye before turning around and marrying the Count if

103

she knew we were plotting in the other direction," Dorothy Simpson warned.

"Would that our approval of Waltham send her to Charles Cavanaugh!" Lord Shelton exclaimed. "But I must say that it is easier when you and I are on the same side!"

"Indeed," Lady Simpson said, "though we have done all we can for one night."

Lord Shelton took his mother-in-law's hand and led her to the stairs, leaving Alcott to extinguish the candles.

In the morning, the Shelton household was visited by Mrs. Lucy James, the Count's married daughter, only six years shy of what would have been Rosanna's mother's age, were dear-hearted Lila still alive.

Rosanna descended in high spirits, anxious to meet her "daughter-in-law," she thought laughingly. She had convinced herself after a good night's sleep, that Charles Cavanaugh was no threat to her planned life with the Count and decided to put him completely out of her mind.

"Good morrow," Rosanna extended her hand to Lucy James. "How was your passage from Somersetshire?"

"It was less than harrowing although I did not plan to arrive quite so late into the night," Lucy explained as she removed her white gloves.

Lucy James was not an unhandsome woman, not beautiful by any stretch of the imagination, but not unpleasant either. She did little to improve on what nature had given her, Rosanna noticed. Her hair was a straight bob and the grey ran freely through the muddy brown strands. The lines of age had already etched themselves in the corners of her eyes and she wore no kohl to detract from their narrowness. Rosanna felt herself being scrutinized and then, as they sat in the drawing room, was sure Lucy James was sizing it as well. She did not seem unimpressed with what she saw.

"Might I offer you a café-au-lait?" Rosanna asked as Alcott attended to their needs.

"Please," her guest responded in a singularly monotone voice.

"Would you like to discuss the wedding right off or would you prefer to chat?" Rosanna asked when no sound came from her new relation.

"Should not Lady Simpson be present?"

"Gregory has told you all about my family then," Rosanna inferred.

"Father has told me ... the essentials," Lucy answered, leaving her hostess to wonder precisely what was the gist of that conversation.

Was Lucy shocked at the difference in their ages, Rosanna wondered? It would certainly take some time getting used to all the way around ....

"I believe that my grandmother will join us presently, and we will have the benefit of her thoughts on this matter," Rosanna said.

"Lady Shelton, I must asked you a frank question—do you love my father?" Lucy asked with concern.

"Mrs. James, your father and I respect each other a great deal—"

"But if you do not love each other, why are you seeking so permanent an alliance?"

"We have agreed upon a marriage by contract. We agree on most of the same things—though I do not understand why he did not explain this to you. We believe that we can improve the quality of each other's lives by our union. Your father wishes a male heir and I would like to have a child someday as well," Rosanna explained.

Rosanna felt that Lucy had, in these few moments, taken an intense dislike to her. Unknowingly, Lucy James was of the same opinion as Lady Simpson and Lord Shelton, that her father's marriage to this woman would be a grave error. She had, however, little idea of how to stop it.

"Have you brought your guest list with you?" Rosanna asked, hoping this would ease the tension of their first meeting.

That task was readily adopted by Dorothy Simpson who entered the room in the highest spirits.

"Lucy James? It is an honor to meet you—but, my, don't you look just like your papa?"

"How do you do, Lady Simpson?" Lucy asked with the same cold indifference that punctuated her conversation with Rosanna.

"Very well, now that you have arrived in town and might assist us with these proceedings," Lady Simpson answered.

"Lucy was about to give me her list of invitations," Rosanna said.

And Mrs. James might very well have done so, had Charles Cavanaugh not appeared on their doorstep, asking to see Lady Shelton.

Rosanna's heart began to flutter upon hearing his name. She did not quite know what to say, with Mrs. James' ears perked. For the second time, Lady Simpson saved the day.

"If it is urgent, Alcott, you must show him in and Mrs. James will accompany me on a tour of the house," Lady Simpson said, making Sir Cavanaugh out to be a man of business, or the like, for her guest's benefit. "It is perhaps not a problem he wishes to share with us all."

Rosanna was too stunned by this turn of events to realize what her grandmother had just done, or why. It was all she could do to smooth her skirt and pinch her cheeks before Sir Cavanaugh was ushered into the room and Mrs. James ushered out with only the briefest of introductions. But when Rosanna's eyes met his, a new stream of life filled her.

"You are lovely as ever, Lady Rose," Sir Charles said, taking her hand. "I would have liked to bid your grandmother a good morrow, but she did whisk her friend from the room with such speed one would think she did not want her guest's presence to be noticed."

"Mrs. James is a shy woman up from the country," Rosanna said the first thing that popped into her head. "She is in London for only a few days and it has been so long since they have spoken."

"I see," Charles said, not entirely sure he understood, or wanted to. "But how are you this morning? Has your headache dissipated?"

"Yes," Rosanna said, certain that if she had one now it would vanish with the mere sight of him.

"I hope it did not keep you from enjoyment last evening. I had a most pleasing time at your friend's house," he told her.

"Is she not a friend of yours as well?" Christina asked.

"I believe that the late Lord Chattering was an acquaintance of my father's and that my invitation came from that source. I would not have so readily accepted, but I knew that you would be there," he assured her. "It is no secret about town that you and Lady Chattering are fast friends."

"Does my presence at a soiree mean so much to

you?" Rosanna asked boldly, seized by a power that released her good senses from her mind every time she found herself within the range of Sir Charles Cavanaugh's touch.

"Rosanna, you cannot be unaware that your company pleases me greatly. I should like to say that, though we are each past the age to need the approval of our parents, I am also pleased by the fact that both our fathers encourage our friendship. I should like to know if you would not mind my calling upon you."

"Sir Cavanaugh, you flatter me," Rosanna said, restraining her eagerness.

"There's no flattery about it, Rosanna Shelton. I am hopelessly in love with you," he said, the Irish passion rising in his voice. "In Ireland, the women who have fire and spunk, as you do, are often tomboyish and a bit vulgar, but you are always feminine, soft and warm, proud of your opinions and free to express them. A rare combination that I cannot hope to be immune to for long."

"Charles, I do not know what to say to such words of love," Rosanna answered. She was not free to return them, though her heart begged her do so.

"Say nothing yet," he insisted. "I would not have your headache return. I will call on you tomorrow." He drew her hand next to his heart. "Can you feel my passion?" With his Irish curls tossed about his head, he took his leave.

As she heard the front door of her house close, Rosanna's heels once again touched earth. She realized as quickly that she was letting herself fall deeper and deeper into a chasm whose bottom could only prove painful. Lucy's purse and gloves poised on the sofa table reminded her that she was burning both ends of the candle and that the flames were catching up to each other. How had her grandmother the presence of mind to scurry Lucy from the room? Lady Simpson was not blind to her feelings for Charles, of that Rosanna was certain. How could she continue with these wedding plans, she wondered? How could she ever face her Grandmama's eyes again?

Rosanna could have little idea how much of Dorothy Simpson's support she possessed, of the heart-to-heart talk she and Lucy James were having in her sitting room.

"My dear, you have said very little since your arrival," Lady Simpson began, "yet I can sense you disapprove of this marriage."

"In all frankness, Lady Simpson—since you bring it up—I cannot hide my feelings very well. My opinion has no bearing on the question of your granddaughter for she is a beautiful and polite young lady. But I believe that it would be wholly inappropriate for her to marry my father. I do not doubt a genuine affection exists between them, but hearing each talk of the other, I cannot say it is enough on which to base a marriage.

"I should tell you of my own marriage, for that failure is partly to blame for my view. You see, I, like your granddaughter, chose to marry in my youth, before I was sure of myself and my own character. For Rosanna to marry a man so much more set in his ways than she, when she does not yet know her truest desires ... I cannot give my blessing," Lucy James confessed.

"Have you spoken to your father on this subject?" Lady Simpson asked, hatching in her mind a plot whereby Lord Waltham could be persuaded to break the agreement.

"I have not had the opportunity, yet I can sense that he is quite convinced of the propriety of this course of action. If I am correct in assuming you agree with me, the matter rests solely in our hands . . . unless you think Rosanna could be persuaded in another direction," Lucy James said.

"Mrs. James, not only do I agree with you, and think highly of your father, I am positive that Rosanna's true interests lie in a completely opposite direction, one of which she is perhaps not yet even aware," Lady Simpson admitted. "It is, in fact, the one issue upon which her father and I are of accord."

"Father and daughter are even less frequently of accord," Mrs. James said, of her own relationship. "Father hardly ever sees eye to eye with me—my sharing this opinion with him would aid in no way."

"Then we must find another tack," Lady Simpson said. "I propose that we put our thinking caps on at once and endeavor to conjure a way to turn this situation around."

Both women shook their hands in concurrence.

As if Rosanna did not have enough dilemma caught between two suitors, the Baronet Playmore decided to fortify his offensive, and began calling on her nearly as frequently as did Sir Cavanaugh. The proximity with which their paths crossed set Rosanna on tenterhooks every morn and afternoon. Though she had requested Alcott accept his card and turn him away, she was troubled by his frequent appearances on her threshold as though she knew danger was imminent.

The Baronet quickly tired of being put off and soon devised a new strategem. Rosanna was expected at Lady Wolverton's for bridge, siding with

Alana Quentin against her hostess and Christina Chattering as she did once each fortnight. On this particular evening, Alana was stricken with a horrid malaise.

"I would have had to scotch the whole affair," Lady Wolverton said as she led Rosanna into her London drawing room, "had not the Baronet Playmore called upon me this afternoon, and upon hearing of my daughter's illness offered to make up our fourth."

"Indeed," Rosanna said, feeling an ache in the center of her stomach. "Was he lingering long at *your* doorstep?"

"Rosanna, darling, surely you don't think Gregory will mind," her future sister-in-law assured her.

"Lady Shelton, you do not worry after my talent at the game, do you?" the Baronet inquired without so much as a how-do-you-do.

"I hear tell you are an admirable player," she answered, wondering if her hostess or the already arrived Christina Chattering knew they spoke not of bridge.

"You will allow the substitution, won't you, Rosanna? I would so hate to cancel the match," Lady Wolverton said. "I couldn't ask another soul—you know my husband is at our estate in Northampton this week."

"I will allow it," Rosanna said as she watched the Baronet tip his head towards her as though they shared an intimacy. A match of bridge does not a liaison make, she wanted to tell him.

As chance would have it, Rosanna and Playmore took the game, thanks to his clever bidding and her skill as a player. She congratulated him when they found themselves alone in the drawing room, Lady Wolverton looking in on her ailing daughter and Christina making some repairs in her *maquillage*—unneeded, the Baronet had insisted as she quit the room.

"You played admirably," Rosanna admitted. "If I had known you were so skilled a dummy, I would have engaged you as my partner long ago," she added, fully realizing the sting of her words.

"I think that I shall turn the hand on you, Lady Shelton," he said. "I should like to declare myself to you and your happiness."

"Lord Playmore, that is wholly unnecessary," Rosanna answered, tossing off his offer casually. "You must know by now that I have concluded a marriage agreement with Count Waltham, our hostess's own brother."

"I feel that can only ease the way towards our own union; for what shall you do with a man old enough to be your father, than to take a young lover who can please you in a myriad of ways on which your innocent mind has not yet dreamed?"

"Lord Playmore, I shall have to join my Lady Wolverton above if you continue to speak in such wild distraction and see to it that you are never allowed in this home again," she promised.

"Why do you think me distracted, dear lady?" he asked, dropping to his knees at her feet. "Can you but know it is the passion I feel in my heart? I have been in love with you these past weeks ... months ... waiting patiently for the slightest encouragement to put forth my suit. And now, to learn that the cloak of marriage will protect us even as we are seen together about town, I thought 'twas past praying for!" he exclaimed.

"I fear it will come as a shocking disappointment to you, Lord Playmore, but I do not marry the

Count so that you and I might have a secret liaison in safety," Rosanna said.

"But surely that is precisely what promoted you to such a decision, on Lady Chattering's famous example," he said. "It will offer you all the freedom your virginity denies."

"Lord Playmore, that is the outside of enough!" Rosanna protested with great vehemence. "You will take your leave at once!"

"You will think on my proposal at great length. I will visit you on the morrow," he threatened. "I am certain that after a night's reflection, you will be pleased with what I offer: myself, an artful lover and a pleasing escort." With that he took his leave, stopping once in the foyer to tip his hat to the returning Christina Chattering.

"What was that all about?" she asked Rosanna, taking a seat beside her on the sofa. "Why did he leave so abruptly?" She barely had a chance to speak with him alone—only a flirting glance exchanged.

"I haven't the faintest idea," Rosanna answered, dismissing the topic. But she could not dismiss it as easily from her mind. She was not sure why, but she did not take Lord Playmore's threat as lightly as she would have liked.

Rosanna Shelton had the most distinct impression that the Baronet Playmore would stop short perhaps of only murder before making this conquest that had become, evidently, an obsession. If only she could interest him in another. But who? she asked herself.

"You look so troubled," Christina said to her young friend. "Might I be of some assistance?"

Chapter Eight

To usher Sir Cavanaugh into the drawing room under any circumstances, was Alcott's standing order.
Rosanna did not suspect, however, that Sir Charles
would arrive during the latter portion of the Baronet's impassioned soliloquy early on the morrow....

Lord Playmore had arrived a full quarter hour
earlier and had begun to use whatever reason would
aid Rosanna in succumbing to his advances, the
desired climax of their acquaintance, without stopping short of blackmail.

Rosanna had asked Alcott to send the Baronet
away upon first learning of his presence, but when
the butler returned with the ominous message, "Tell
your mistress she will see me at once or regret
having done so at her leisure," Rosanna was forced
to acquiesce. Lord Playmore was admitted, and Al-

cott instructed to remain within earshot—regardless of what the Baronet had come to say, Rosanna knew it would go no further than her trusted servant.

"I thank the heavens that your heart took pity on me this day," he had begun and flung himself at Rosanna's feet.

"Come, Lord Playmore," Rosanna had answered, trying to conceal her laughter. "This stance does not suit you at all."

"You are wrong, fair lady, I belong at your feet where I can worship you."

"Lord Playmore, I have never given you any reason to believe that I would want your attention or give you leave to present yourself in my drawing room in such an affected state."

Rosanna was not as taken aback as she had been the morning of the hunt, now secure in her own home, her bastion. She was even a bit amused, she fancied, by the Baronet's *mise-en-scène*.

"I have endeavored to win your affections these past weeks, Lady Shelton. I mean to have you," he insisted.

Rosanna checked her tone. "I do not love you, Lord Playmore, and I am afraid that precludes any further discussion."

"You cannot convince me that you love Lord Waltham, and yet you plan to marry—a fact which, oddly enough, you choose to keep secret. Perhaps there is someone from whom you wish to conceal the truth. Perhaps it is Sir Charles Cavanaugh."

The expression that then appeared on Rosanna's face confirmed what Playmore had said. He had so shocked her that she could not stop her emotions from betraying her.

"You will reconsider the offer I make. I am

certain, if you do not give me satisfaction, that I can find an opportune moment to inform his lordship of this interesting development in your life," the Baronet threatened.

"If I am to marry Lord Waltham in less than a month," Rosanna said as she had regained her presence of mind, "what possibly can lead you to believe I hope to keep this happy news from my friend, Charles Cavanaugh?"

"I cannot know," he answered, "unless you have your doubts about this marriage. But I do not think that, even if you should call off the wedding, the future Earl would consider it very sporting of you to have let him play the suitor to a woman affianced."

Indeed not, Rosanna thought to herself, and believed she was squarely in the Baronet's trap. But she could not succumb to his advances, nor could she send him out into the streets of London bearing such tidings as her impending marriage.

"I must have time to consider what you have said," Rosanna answered him as Charles Cavanaugh was ushered inside the Shelton home. Unknown to Rosanna, he witnessed Lord Playmore's final plea: "My heart breaks that I must talk with you in such a fashion," he said.

"Then rise to your feet and spare yourself further humiliation," Rosanna implored him. "There is no more to be said."

"Indeed there is, dear lady," he answered, still on his knees. "How I find your beauty exquisite, your charm irresistible, your smile so inviting, your laugh so pleasing—you are more than any man could hope for, a dream come true," and he clutched at her hands.

"Lord Playmore, your self-respect," Rosanna chided him.

She was startled by the sound of her butler's voice.

"Might I be of some assistance?"

Both Rosanna and the Baronet turned to face Alcott standing to the left of Sir Charles Cavanaugh. No one knew who was more embarrassed, Sir Cavanaugh for interrupting this tender scene, Rosanna for having Charles think that she cared for this display, Lord Playmore for being caught on his knees by a man he considered his rival, or Alcott for obeying his mistress's wishes though he had sensed this particular circumstance was unique in the extreme.

"I will take my leave now," the Baronet said. "Think carefully of what I have said," he added before tossing a perfunctory look at Sir Cavanaugh.

"Alcott, will you see to it that the Baronet finds his way *out*," Rosanna instructed the servant and then turned to her guest.

"Are you accustomed to such outbursts from a suitor?" Sir Charles asked, grinning, hoping to end the awkwardness of Lord Playmore's display.

"Frankly, no," Rosanna said. "And Lord Playmore is hardly one of my suitors. His presence here today was unexpected and unencouraged."

"You protest at great length," Charles told her. "I think you must be aware of Lord Playmore's interest—I could not help but take note of his overly solicitous behavior at Lady Chattering's the other evening."

"Is that so?" Rosanna asked coolly. "I had not noticed anything more than a friendly interest."

"He was hardly terse, Rosanna," he said, calling her by her given name for the first time.

"Sir Cavanaugh," she was purposefully formal, "one would think you the slightest bit . . . jealous."

"Perhaps only the slightest bit," he confessed and took her hands in his. "Are you certain I have not cause to be?"

"Certainly not from Lord Playmore's direction," she said honestly, but added no more. "It is unfortunate that you were forced to suffer his conversation. I hope you were not excessively annoyed." She hoped to learn how much he had heard.

"I heard only his closing argument," Sir Cavanaugh admitted, "though his first dialogue must have been equally engaging."

"You cannot believe it," Rosanna said. "It was an artless tirade, a product of his lusty propensities. He is hardly a peer, lacking in many of the social graces."

"It is worse than his birth; he is an adorer of women, and they will be his downfall. But we need not let him be the focus of our conversation," he suggested.

"Shall we sit then?" Rosanna asked, leading him to the sofa.

"Yes," Charles answered, but did not appear to have dismissed the subject of the Baronet as quickly as he would have liked.

"Is there something you wished to say?" Rosanna asked, unsettled by his pensive mood.

"Only that you must know the Baronet and I are very different men, that where he seeks to garner the attention of many women, I search for one. Where he loses interest after the chase, I am forever captivated. I seek a woman with whom to share my life, to marry and raise a family. Those are the traditional values I learned as a child, fortified by the very essence of life in Ireland where family is paramount," he explained.

"What else do you hold important?" she asked, anxious to learn all she could about this handsome, captivating man.

"That it is important to marry someone who has a comparable upbringing; who shares your beliefs; who will place the man she loves before any and all other concerns. It is rare to find a woman who will be as dedicated to her husband as she is to maintaining her social standing, although I must say it is easier for those with a shared heritage.

"It is important to carry on one's father's lineage," he said, "to preserve his place in our society and the order of things."

"How fortunate that both our fathers hold the title of Earl," Rosanna said before realizing how telling a statement that was, inappropriate in view of her alliance to Count Waltham.

"I hope you do not play with your words, Lady Shelton, I am not used to such candor. Honesty is most important to me as well. Nothing can exist without it. It signifies respect and courtesy. If you are honest, you can fear nothing. Do you see?"

"Clearly," Rosanna answered, applying his words to not only their friendship but the one she had erroneously begun with the Count. She had betrayed both men and herself as well. She had never believed she could meet a man with whom she would want to spend her whole life; instead she had planned her life around her friends and chosen a man who best accomodated it, and now realized that what she wanted in her heart was a man to whom she could devote her life. She began not only to doubt her interest in Lord Waltham but the importance of her friendship with Lady Wolverton and those in her circle, all of whom cared little for

119

family, preferring to set the styles and confine themselves to a precious circle few could join.

"I did not mean to land you so deep in thought," Sir Charles said. "Nor saddle you with another headache."

"You do no such thing," Rosanna assured him. "You have given me great cause for reflection, and that is good."

"I wonder if your relations would agree.... How is dear Lady Simpson and your father, Lord Shelton?" he asked. "I was hoping to bid them a good day."

"Grandmother has locked herself away in her sitting room this morning, and Father is not yet returned for luncheon. Would you join us when he does?" Rosanna asked, not wishing him to leave her side.

"I am saddened to say I cannot. But you must offer them my regrets. I have spent more time than I planned in your pleasing company—I fear I will be tardy for an appointment, such is the magical spell you cast," he said with great ardor. "I hope I have not kept you from something more important."

"Indeed you have not," she assured him. "I have enjoyed your visit immensely."

"Then you would not be disappointed if I should call again soon?"

"No, I would not," she said as he took his leave.

Rosanna fell into a pensive mood anew and sought out the solitude of her own apartment. But her footsteps on the stair did not go unnoticed by Lady Simpson who called her to her sitting room.

"You have had a goodly number of visitors this day," Grandmother Dorothy said.

"More than I am well used to."

"And was Charles Cavanaugh among them?"

"Yes," Rosanna said, unable to hide the smile the remembrance of his visit precipitated.

"Is he the one who has left your head in the clouds?" her grandmother pursued the subject.

"We spoke of many serious things today—tradition, family, marriage . . ."

"Did you happen to mention your imminent marriage to Lord Waltham?"

"I . . . actually there was . . . No, I did not," Rosanna confessed.

"Rosanna, perhaps you would not mind my asking a very presumptuous question, yet one you might well know to answer . . ."

"Yes?"

"Do you think you could fall in love with Charles Cavanaugh?"

"Yes."

"Are you already in love with Charles Cavanaugh?"

"Yes!"

"Oh, dear!"

"Yes!"

"You are in quite a muddle, granddaughter, in love with one man and attached to another. It is not an issue that could be settled over a cup of tea," her grandmother said.

"What am I to do? I feel so peculiar."

"Because you are beginning to realize that your arrangement with Lord Waltham is not sufficient to afford you the happiness you desire, child. Well, you must let me think on it while I dress for the Opera—but you have not forgotten that tonight the Count and his daughter have invited us to see the presentation of *Il Barbiere di Siviglia?*"

"Yes, with Señor Garcia," Rosanna said, trying to muster some enthusiasm. But the prospect of

121

spending the evening with Lucy James was less than promising.

"We will take some time to ponder these matters and draw certain conclusions," her grandmother suggested.

"You are right. I should do a lot of thinking on this subject for, to tell true, my heart is quite divided. As I have never fallen in love before, I cannot be certain this is it," Rosanna said. But if it is not love, she thought silently, what else could explain the pounding of her heart within her bosom whenever she thought of Sir Cavanaugh, and the ache in her belly when she thought of Lord Waltham?

When Rosanna quit the room, Dorothy Simpson smiled to herself. Not only was Rosanna smitten by Sir Cavanaugh, she had also begun to doubt her feelings for Lord Waltham. Lord Shelton would find these events rare good news. And if they were having such good fortune with Rosanna, there was no telling what headway Mrs. James was making with her father.

Late that evening, as she and her father were enjoying an aperitif before adjourning to the Sheltons, was the first chance Lucy had to broach the subject of the marriage with her father.

"I met with Rosanna yesterday, as you suggested. We had a pleasant time as we discussed the wedding plans," she began.

"Is not Rosanna a marvel for a woman of her tender years?" Lord Waltham interrupted her to ask.

"She is very sophisticated," his daughter admitted. "But I feel I must tell you I am not yet convinced you are making the correct decision."

122

"How can you say that when you have only known the girl for two days?"

"Because she is precisely that, a young *girl* whose head is beginning to turn in a hundred different directions, and who might soon grow tired of her older husband whose demands increase with the passing of each year." Lucy knew that the words were harsh, but saw no other way to gain her father's attention.

"Do you think your father has one foot in the grave?"

"Of course not," she quickly answered. "But she is barely out of the cradle, if we are to make comparisons."

"Rosanna is hardly a babe, nor so young and innocent that she is not to be trusted to know what she wants," he insisted. "Surely she has had the pick of the season's eligibles for the last three years. And if she has not chosen one of them, it is because they fall short of her standards, where I do not."

"I wish I could believe it, Father, but I have reasons to suspect that, not only do her interests wander, but lay specifically at the door of one future Earl whom I met at the Shelton's yesterday morning!"

"And whom might that be?" her father asked, that same hint of jealousy as the other night at Lady Chattering's appearing in his eyes.

Lucy realized that she was taking matters a bit further than Lady Simpson would have liked, though she knew Rosanna's grandmother wished her do all she could to remove Lord Waltham from the young girl's life, she did not wish her granddaughter's reputation tarnished. But Mrs. James knew her father well. Mere suggestion would not go very far

123

towards altering his plan. Facts—names, if necessary, certainly circumstances which could be verified, would well-accomplish the desired goal.

"He is Sir Charles Cavanaugh, son of the Earl of Clifford," Lucy admitted.

The Count paused for a moment and then said, "I met the Earl and his son the other evening. Lord Cavanaugh is an old and dear friend of Lord Shelton—I find nothing peculiar in the son calling at the Shelton home."

"Do you not find it odd that as soon as Sir Cavanaugh appeared in the Shelton drawing room, Lady Simpson took my by the hand and led me from the room before the reason for my being there could be learned? I suffered a tour of the house for what seemed to be the sole purpose of allowing Rosanna and Charles a tête-à-tête!" Lucy exclaimed, remembering the discomfort of that situation.

"I cannot believe it, daughter. If Rosanna Shelton was interested in Charles Cavanaugh, a man whose power and financial standing well exceed mine, why did she settle on me?"

"That is a question I cannot answer, Father," Lucy James confessed. "But perhaps Rosanna or Charles can. I suggest you take up the matter with one or the other ... or both, should you find them together."

"Daughter, your words sting. It is cruel disappointment to hear you voice such strenuous objection to my plan for happiness. To think of the lengths you reach to discredit Lady Shelton!"

"Father, it is that I love you that I wish you to answer this charge, and derive only joy from your union. I do not think it is too much to ask Rosanna, or Sir Cavanaugh, after their friendship. I would not have you a cuckold before the vows are exchanged," she said.

"That is disrespectful talk, Lucy Waltham James, and I'll not suffer any more of it!" he vowed. "You will put this matter aside as I'll not have it discussed at the Opera." He grew so cross with his daughter, he did not think he would speak with her again during the duration of her stay in London.

Indeed, the next time Mrs. James spoke, it was in a whisper, and to Lady Dorothy Simpson. Upon their arrival at the opera box, each confessed their progress to the other.

"My success has been limited to persuading Father to consider the sagacity of marriage to one so youthful and ingénue," Lucy said in half-truth. "And you?"

"Rosanna now questions the whole idea of marriage to your father, feeling that her emotions might be better kindled in another quarter."

Lucy smiled, taking this as conformation of her own suspicion that Rosanna was interested in Sir Cavanaugh.

"Perhaps we can have the situation remedied by the week's end," Lady Simpson said, putting a smile on Mrs. James's face. She settled back into her opera chair to enjoy the piece.

With the past weeks' excitement, Rosanna could barely remember the gist of the libretto, but when she head Manuel Garcia upon the stage, he brought new meaning to the story and confirmed Rosanna's doubts about a young girl's marriage to an older man. She grew thankful that *her* father was not forcing her hand. As she watched the heroine of the opera fall in love with the young, handsome

125

suitor, she could think only of Sir Charles Cavanaugh.

"Garcia is as wonderful as promised," the Count whispered to Rosanna. "Do you not agree?"

"Indeed I do. He makes the meaning behind the story so clear." She was consumed by the cognizance of the error she would be making were she to go through with the marriage. In a moment, her path was laid out before her. To confess all to Charles as soon as possible. If he forgave her, it would be miraculous. If he did not, so be it; at least she would be able to tell Lord Waltham they could not go ahead, and save herself from that tragedy even if she could not claim the love of Charles Cavanaugh in his place.

Rosanna was grateful that her father had declined Lady Wolverton's invitation for a cold repast at her apartment after the presentation. She wished to return home at once to pen Sir Cavanaugh a note, requesting his presence at tea on the morrow.

Rosanna persuaded the family groom to bring the note round to Cavanaugh house. It was past midnight and he was not to expect an answer, but merely to slip it under the door. Rosanna had little doubt that he would accept, might even visit her in the morning as was his wont these past few days, she thought, and fell asleep thinking of him.

That Charles Cavanaugh had an appointment at the early hour of nine was perhaps the greatest stroke of back luck that fate could have dealt him, and set about a chain of misunderstandings concerning his friendship with Rosanna that might perhaps never be set to right again.

Chapter Nine

"I wager a hundred pounds," said the red-headed Sir Ivan Bowles.

"A mere hundred?" Lord Wrent could not believe his ears. "Two-fifty or nothing!"

"Two-fifty it shall be then—are we agreed?" Robert Daniels asked. "Good! Shall we give our notes to Winston?" he suggested, indicating the able-bodied manservant who catered to the needs of Peppernell's Oak Room members.

"What are you gadabouts up to now?" Sir Cavanaugh asked as he joined the group. His friend Mr. Daniels had just placed the scripts on Winston's tray.

"Where've you been off to?" Robert Daniels countered, as he placed a hand on the butler's wrist, letting him know he should wait for perhaps another note. "We've been lacking in your counsel this morning."

"I had to see to a business matter concerning my father's holdings—but when did you ever need my counsel?" he asked his crony.

"Since an interesting bit of news broke just this day," Bob Daniels said. "And we've been placing a little wager on its va-li-di-ty! As it concerns you—indirectly, of course—we thought your opinion might influ-en-ce the odds," he added in auditory tones.

"What are you speaking of?" Sir Charles asked, confounded by his friend's double talk.

"Lady Rosanna Shelton."

"Lady Rose? What could you be wagering up-on that fair head?"

"You haven't heard then—she's engaged to marry Count Gregory Waltham, relation of Lord Wolverton," Lord Wrent enlightened him.

"Engaged? Count Waltham?" Sir Charles echoed incredulous.

"Indeed, Bonnie Charlie!" Lord Wrent repeated, bellowing.

"Hold on, Wrent," Bob Daniels said, aware of the saddened expression on Charles Cavanaugh's face. "I think Charlie's smitten by the—we only meant to have a bit of fun . . . had no idea you were truly taken with her . . . ."

"Taken with her?" he asked, now trying to hide any discomfort he was feeling. "I did not know the lady well enough," he insisted.

"Then would you care to add your two-fifty quid to the kitty?" Lord Wrent asked before he saw Bob Daniels give him a silencing nod. It was too late.

"What are the terms of the wager?" Charles asked with keen interest.

"We bet whether or not it will come off. The odds are three to one it won't," Lord Wrent said in a much less enthusiastic tone.

"I will bet against you all that it will!" Sir Cavanaugh challenged.

"That is foolhardy, Charles. There are four of us now, and no telling how many others will put in theirs," Bob Daniels warned. "I can't allow it—'twouldn't be sporting."

"I said, I'll take all," he reiterated, thinking it would be worth two-fifty times ten to be found wrong.

"It is overly generous of you, Bonnie Charlie," Lord Wrent said.

"You've still time to change your mind," Sir Ivan offered, but was turned down.

Bob Daniels studied his friend, wondering precisely how smitten he was by the dark-haired beauty. A mite, he suspected. His suspicions were confirmed when he heard the tone with which Sir Cavanaugh addressed Lord Waltham as he appeared in the doorway of the Oak Room.

"Good morrow, Sir Cavanaugh," the Count said.

"Good morrow," Sir Charles answered. "Your excessive good humor must have to do with your engagement to Lady Shelton. Allow me to offer my sincerest congratulations." He extended his hand.

"Thank you, Sir Cavanaugh," the older man said. "Might I impose upon your good nature for a moment?"

"How might I help you?"

"Could we perhaps adjourn to my study

above?" the Count asked. "Perhaps we could talk over a cup of coffee, unless you find it not too early for something more fortifying . . ."

As they quit the room, the voice of speculation rose up again, leaving one to wonder if Lord Peter Wrent might not offer a wager on the subject of the departeds' dialogue.

"How can I be of assistance?" Sir Cavanaugh asked as he settled into a leather armchair.

"I am about to ask you a most forward question—perhaps you can attribute it to an old man's folly. I have many more doubts and suspicions than a young gentleman filled with all the naive optimism the heavens can offer. There is no secret about the vast difference in my age and that of Rosanna—it can be even greater if her interests run to someone younger . . . I am asking you, Sir Cavanaugh, for confirmation that I have chosen my bride wisely," the Count explained.

"How can I answer you?"

"By telling me that your acquaintance with Rosanna is merely familial, a direct consequence of your fathers' friendship," he said bluntly.

"It is most assuredly nothing more than that," Charles replied without hesitation. "You have my word on that." He had convinced himself that whatever interest he might have had in Lady Rose had been crushed by the news of her engagement. To think that she had allowed him to court her with all the ardor of a boy in his first breath of love! he thought to himself. And all the while she planned to be affianced to the man who now sat beside him. How could she have toyed with him so cruelly? he wondered. A woman with so sweet and kind a face . . . such a cruel deception is Woman capable of, he mused wistfully. Had he been less of a gentleman, he would have cursed the day he met her.

"You have appeased the mind of a nervous old man," Count Waltham said with unaccustomed vulnerability.

"Think not on it, for it would be foolhardy not to question the rightness of a marriage, particularly to one so different from yourself," Sir Cavanaugh said and could not help but be reminded of his last conversation with Rosanna—of how she had agreed with all he had said on that very subject, *all the while thinking of another!* It pained him to sit with Waltham; he reminded Sir Charles of Rosanna all the more. He asked to be excused on the occasion of a prior engagement and left Peppernell's at once.

Lord Waltham was pleased. He wished to return home to his daughter and give her a sound talking to. It would not do at all for her to put doubts in his mind and create any kind of dissention between him and his fiancée. Lucy could revisit London in time for the wedding along with Mr. James, but the Count was certain her presence was not needed for its preparation.

"Father, why is the upstairs maid packing my trunk?" Lucy James asked her father later that day.

"Because you are returning to your husband—I'll not have you here causing trouble."

"What do you mean? That my own father is putting me out?" she protested.

"It is for your own good. If you should try once again to put doubts in my mind about my bride—"

"Have you at least spoken to Sir Cavanaugh as I suggested?" she demanded, crossing her arms over her bosom.

"Indeed I have," the Count answered.

"And what did he tell you?" she asked, hoping his anger was in response to his fears having been confirmed.

"That I worry needlessly. He explicitly denied any but a friendly interest in dear Rosanna. Nothing more!"

"And you believed him?" his daughter asked, not believing her ears. How could have Charles Cavanaugh deliberately denied the infatuation he had plainly shown to her that morning at the Shelton house?

"Why should I not? If he loved Rosanna, he would not have passed this opportunity to tell me and stop this marriage."

Fortunately, Lucy stood directly in front of a cushioned chair in her father's drawing room for she did near faint dead away at the sound of these words. How could her suspicions have betrayed her? she wondered. How could her once keen perceptions have dulled overnight? She would have sworn on her favored stack of Bibles that Rosanna and Charles were in love .... And now what could she hope to accomplish? Her father was sending her home to Somersetshire, leaving himself more vulnerable than before.

"Why do you seem so stunned?" the Count asked. "Do you think your father such an ogre no woman would want to claim him for a husband?"

"No, Father, no. It is only that I was—" Lucy realized she could go no further, could not blacken Lady Simpson's name by saying that she had confirmed her own theory. "But must I leave London? Couldn't I stay on until the wedding?" she asked, hoping for more time.

"No. I'll not have any more unhappiness from you," he said though in a more lenient voice.

"Father, you talk as though you were in the first throes of love," she chided him, "a schoolboy walking mindlessly into—"

"That is enough, Lucy. I know as well as you the truer circumstances of my alliance with Rosanna, but that does not mean I must treat it like any other business transaction, at least for Rosanna's sake. It is to be her first wedding," he reminded his daughter who threw up her arms.

"Father, I implore you to let me stay," Lucy said.

"It is out of the question, daughter," he stood firm.

"But I would not try to interfere. I would be a help to you. Surely you need someone to ready the house for Rosanna," Lucy proposed, trying to think of any plausible argument that would allow her to remain in London, after all, she could hardly scheme with Lady Simpson from Somersetshire.

"It is not necessary—Rosanna has comissioned fabric makers to design new upholsteries and craftsmen to create new furnishings. Those matters are well in hand. No, no, there is no reason for your continued residence here. You may return the day before the wedding, and not a moment sooner. Besides, your husband sorely misses you, I am certain," Lord Waltham said.

"Father, you are making a mistake," she said, shaking her head regretfully.

"I have heard enough, Lucy, dear," he said as he walked to where she sat. He kissed her on both cheeks and wished her a pleasant journey home before he left the room.

133

"Confound it!" she exclaimed, digging her heels into the Persian carpet.

The carpet beneath Rosanna's feet was being worn away as she paced the drawing room. She had been waiting for Sir Cavanaugh since three and it was now close to six, with no sign of him yet. Under any other circumstances, she would have thought he had been detained by matters of business. But Rosanna's intuition insisted that his absence was due to a far more serious reason.

Could he have learned the truth? she wondered. But from what source? The possibility seemed mere conjecture, but what else could have kept him away?

Rosanna's heart began to throb when Alcott presented himself, announcing she had a visitor.

"Tis you, Christina," she said dejectedly as Lady Chattering appeared.

"What a most unkind reception—I am sorry I disappoint you," her guest said.

"I should be disappointed were it anyone save—"

"Charles Cavanaugh?" Christina finished the sentence for her.

"How did you divine it?" Rosanna asked.

"I am afraid that I know more than you are going to care to hear. But I would not have you learn this news from any other," her friend said.

"What has happened?"

"Gaylord has told me a most distressing tale, confirmed by more than one source.... We must believe it is the truth. Rosanna, this is..."

"Why do you hesitate?" Rosanna asked fearfully.

"Because I do not wish to hurt you, and hurt

134

you will be if you love Charles Cavanaugh as I suspect," Christina warned.

"I suspect I do," Rosanna gave the awaited answer. "And until a few hours ago, I thought I had reason to believe my feelings were returned. But how did you learn of it?"

"A close friend knows when something is afoot," Christina answered, not giving away Lord Shelton's part in the intrigue.

"I suppose I was quite transparent at your party... even the first time we met," Rosanna confessed. "But from the tone of your voice, I guess that means little now."

"Rosanna, his friends at Peppernell's, that fashionable club," she said sarcastically, "were in the process of placing bets on whether your marriage to Lord Waltham would come off! I am afraid Charles Cavanaugh surprised them and learned of your betrothal from most unsympathetic lips. To cap the scene, Waltham appeared for a short, private interview. Gaylord could not ascertain what was said, but feels confident that Waltham was asking after Sir Cavanaugh's interest in you. If you have been expecting him today, I can only suspect that he fears he has lost you to the Count."

"He knows that I have lied to him, Christina. The content of the lie only worsens my deceit," Rosanna said. "He will never forgive me. Why did I not tell him, you must be thinking. I was afraid I would lose him. And now that he as heard the truth from another, my worst fears are confirmed.... Who has placed the most, those who think I will marry Waltham or nay?"

"I am afraid Sir Cavanaugh has taken the wager against all his friends that you will," Christina answered in a whisper.

"But you have learned all the facets of this tale!" Rosanna sighed.

"Gaylord is nothing if not thorough . . ."

"At least I know the reason for Charles' absence," Rosanna said. "When sleep eludes me tonight, I will know why."

"Rosanna, it is not too late to break with Waltham and ask Charles' forgiveness," her friend suggested. "If he loves you, he will forgive you."

"No. You are wrong. I have hurt him badly, a hurt that is not easily forgotten or forgiven," Rosanna said.

"Will you abandon him and continue with your marriage plans as though you never met him?" Christina asked, not believing her friend's resignation.

"I see no other path to take."

"Then you will listen to the tale I have to tell you and perhaps see your way more clearly."

"What tale?" Rosanna asked.

"The story of my own life which led to my marrying Lord Chattering," Christina began. "You asked me why the opera *Il Barbiere*, had such an effect on me. It was because it so closely paralleled my past. I, too, was in love with a handsome young man, as was the heroine of the piece. A man who could offer me only his love, no power, no title, no wealth, in fact, a worse existence than I might have had on my own. So what did I do? I rejected the love to marry Lord Chattering because through him I could better myself.

"True, I did grow to love dear Egbert as a friend, but that love could never have equaled one of passion, a love I felt for the other man, lost to me forever. I still mourn the love I tossed away—I doubt I shall have another chance at such happiness. But you—you, Rosanna, you need sacrifice yourself for Lord Waltham. You are not in that desperate condition mixed of poverty and ignoble birth," her friend reminded her.

"Christina, I share your pain and I am so sorry for it," Rosanna commiserated.

"It is a pain that does not dissipate easily. I should not like to think of you wrestling with it five or ten years from now, any more than the hurt you feel today. You still have the chance to remedy the situation. Go to Charles, tell him you have made an error, yes, a grave error, but a human error, one that must be forgiven. You must break with Waltham for certainly you will never love him." Christina's words came from her own heart as well as her promise to Lord Shelton.

"I will write to Charles at once and endeavor to explain what I've done an hope that his love for me is strong enough to forgive me," Rosanna said, "and to understand details more complex than what has been offered him this day."

Chapter Ten

As Rosanna sat at the narrow desk in her sitting room, her pen poised in one hand, the other keeping the blank paper still, she thought back to the first time Charles had called her his Lady Rose. A brief glance in the mirror that hung above the table told her she was more like a wilted rose, sad and dejected. She thought of how he had likened her to a flower and the days of her life to petals, each an adventure holding a secret. She hoped he would see this day's petal as a little misadventure and dismiss it as one small facet, that added to the others made her the woman she was.

That was too poetic a sentiment to write to him, she thought. What would a man prefer? The facts, simply conveyed, without a flourish nor embellishment of any kind. But Rosanna was so distraught that at first she could not even pen the salutation.

Should she write "Dear Charles"? "Sir Cavanaugh"? "Dear Sir Cavanaugh"? So stymied was she that when she began to compose the words and mark them down, she left off the greeting altogether. It did not signify, she knew. There would be many versions of this letter; this was merely the first.

Rosanna explained her great unhappiness with the men who called on her after her come-out at the same time as she felt the need to become established in her own home. She described her meeting with Lord Waltham, her opinion that he met most of her requirements, that she knew love would never be in the offing...

Rosanna tore the paper in two. *It will take him half and hour to reach the part that concerns him if I go on in this vein,* she said aloud. She started the next attempt with an apology, explaining her motivation as fear. "If I had told you of my agreement with Lord Waltham," she wrote, "I should never have been able to learn about you and fall in love with you." She went on to write of all the times she had begun to tell him the truth, but had been afraid that the truth would separate them; that the invitation to tea sent the night before was to tell him all this; that she never meant for him to find out in such a cruel way. "I had ultimately realized that the pain of your lost friendship would be superior only to the shame I felt at hiding this dreadful secret. It was only through our friendship that I learned marrying Lord Waltham was a grave error, we do not belong together. I ask no more than your forgiveness."

Rosanna did not want to encumber the letter with the recounting of any of the other, now unthinkable events that had marked her relationship with the Count. If Charles needed to hear more, she would satisfy his every question. But for now, she could nary be sure he would read this brief apology, much less contend with a longer missive. She read the letter aloud and made countless changes, a word here and there and there and there ... until she was forced to rewrite the whole, slowly and with care.

She left her room in search of the groom and entrusted the letter to his scruffy hands, gave him the swiftest course to Sir Cavanaugh's home, and instructions to place the letter in Sir Cavanaugh's hand alone or, if necessary, his personal manservant.

"Shall I wait for a reply, Lady?" the boy asked, brushing the brown locks from in front of his eyes.

"Only if you are asked to do so," she replied wishfully. "You are not to appear as though you expect one."

Rosanna did not leave the kitchen until the boy returned, nearly an hour later, the letter still between his hands.

"What happened?" she asked, her heart tearing within her breast.

"I did as you requested, handed the letter to his man. I was asked to remain on the kitchen doorstep for a time, 'til he was back with the letter. Said 'Sir Cavanaugh refuses this message,'" the boy recounted, adding the cultured tone of the butler's voice to his tale.

"Perhaps Sir Cavanaugh could not be disturbed," Rosanna searched for an excuse to satisfy her own heart. "We shall try again in the morning ... as soon as you awaken."

"Yes, Lady," the groom said, taking it with him to his room atop the carriage house.

This very same scenario was repeated on the

morrow, with the addition of Sir Cavanaugh's express request that the lad not appear on his doorstep again.

"Indeed," Rosanna pronounced and took the letter from him with trembling fingers. Rosanna pressed it close to her bosom as she walked into the drawing room. She sat upon the sofa as she dissolved into tears.

Rosanna was startled by Alcott's presence. He announced a visitor. Her tears stopped in anticipation, but were renewed when she saw Lord Playmore.

"It is too late for your threats," she said in between sobs. "Sir Cavanaugh knows and will not even listen to my explanation." She waved the letter in her hand. "He no doubt thinks me the worst kind of female, knowing about Waltham and compounding it with the suspicions he has held about you!"

Lord Playmore was too much the romantic not to be moved by this passionate outburst. He knelt at her feet and begged her forgiveness. "Dear Lady, my part in this has added insufferable pain to your torment and I ask for your strictest punishment. I was a selfish boor to thrust my unwanted advances upon you, cruel and insensitive, a brute. Might I take this letter knife and pierce my heart with it?" he asked as he leaned across her to seize the instrument from the console behind the sofa. "Would it ease your grief in any way?" he said and hoped for encouragement.

He was rewarded with the Lady's laughter. "Lord Playmore!" she cried at his frenzied performance.

"At least I have succeeded in staying your sobs if for only a second," he said.

"It will be only a second," she said somberly. "There is no relenting until Charles Cavanaugh walks through that door and forgives me."

"Is that what it will require?" he asked. "If that is all, I will go to him at once and explain to him that he is a fool not to love you."

"He will not listen to you—he has rejected my attempts at explanation . . . twice. I penned it all in this letter which he refuses to read," Rosanna told him.

"I will force him to read it—he will listen to me when I throw myself at his mercy," the Baronet said, aware of his skill at the exercise. "I would go so far as to tell him that my boorish attempts at seduction were what first caused you to seek the protection, the sanctity that marriage to the Count offered," he promised. "I will assume all the blame."

"Part of the blame is yours," Rosanna conceded. "But I cannot deny that lying to Sir Cavanaugh was all my doing."

"Still, I erred," the Baronet said, hungry for a reason to repent.

"I will say that your type, an ardent seducer, often makes it necessary for a woman to seek shelter within marriage, though, I must confess, that does not always stop one of my gender from succumbing to the wily advances of one of yours . . . but that is another matter."

"With your heart torn in two directions, you hardly needed me to add to your dilemma, and for that I will never forgive myself," the Baronet swore.

"Lord Playmore, if I did not know you better, I would say that my tears have touched your heart," Rosanna exclaimed.

"Indeed they have, Lady Shelton," Playmore admitted in a voice so compassionate she would not believe it his. "When one is well used to making the conquest one seeks, one hardly considers the emotions of any other. When one is used to bringing laughter to a lady's lips, it is hard to remember one can as easily cause pain. In truth, I have never attempted to seduce a woman who did not seek it, but a woman of your reputation, a woman who could make me realize that I was toying shamelessly with another's heart. I saw only your beauty, Lady Shelton, not your soul...until today," he argued for her friendship now. "Do not think you have performed a miracle, but I can distinguish a woman of quality from a sea of maids as never before."

"Lord Playmore, there is nothing to convince me that as soon as you leave my home, you will not begin a search for a new conquest," Rosanna said, smiling just the same.

"Not right away," he corrected her.

"What is to detain you?" she asked, amused by his manner.

"I am going to take your letter to Sir Cavanaugh."

"You will never persuade him to read it," she said, unwilling to spring any false hopes.

"I will do my best ... even if that means reading the missive to him. If he is not receiving at home, I will call on him at Peppernell's where he will be unable to ignore me—I am a member, you know," he offered further credentials.

"How can I thank you?"

"Do not thank me until I am successful ... but not even then for it is the least reparation I can make," the Baronet said. "But, out of curiosity, might I ask how he came to learn of the Waltham scheme, if not from you?"

143

"Christina—Lady Chattering—brought word, through her sources, that he had learned of it at Peppernell's," Rosanna explained. "All the world appears to have known, save Charles."

"Lady Chattering, you say?" Playmore caught the part of the answer that most interested him. "And how is she?" he asked, that familiar look of intrigue in his eyes. He had always favored Rosanna above her friend, but now that Lady Shelton was lost as a conquest . . .

"Very well," Rosanna said. "Shall I convey your greeting to her?"

"I should like to reserve that pleasure for myself," he answered mysteriously, "after I have completed my first task of the day."

"Indeed you will," Rosanna said, shaking her head. Lord Playmore will never mend his ways, she thought to herself, but at least he is no longer wagging his tail at me.

The Baronet had succeeded in taking Rosanna's mind from Sir Cavanaugh. But once he departed, she was reminded of her lost love again. There was no error so great, she mused wistfully, as one that cannot be repaired. How rare those were, but how devastating, for there was nothing to do but relive the events in one's mind and feel remorse and no ease.

Rosanna did not wish her father or grandmother to find her with eyes reddened. She went upstairs with the intention of reading a novel for distraction. She had reached her apartment door when Lady Simpson called out to remind her that Lord Waltham would be joining them at dinner and that she might begin to think about her toilette.

"How could I forget?" she called back with regret. But as much as she resented having to entertain him, she knew this was an opportunity to begin to tell him that she could not go through with the marriage.

Rosanna would have given her best bonnet to leave the dinner table prematurely, but she could not. Instead, she sat, hands folded while her father and Lord Waltham exchange their opinions on the Earl of Liverpool, the noted Prime Minister, and even the Regent himself. She could not, however, help noticing that, at frequent intervals, her grandmother redressed her back and put a smile on her face, hoping her granddaughter would emulate her at once. Is my sadness that transparent? she wondered.

When the meal was concluded, Rosanna came to life and asked her fiancé—as she forced herself to think of him—to join her for a stroll through the gardens rather than suffer his lighting that infernal pipe he carried with him.

"Of course," he agreed. "Has something been troubling you, dear? You seemed so unusually silent throughout dinner," he asked as they stepped onto the terrace.

"Yes, Gregory," she said, grateful for this introduction. "Something very grave has been troubling me."

"It is Lucy—I know it. Well, you need not trouble yourself on that score any longer. I have sent her home, certain that she must not be offering her worth in assistance. If the truth be known, she was beginning to grate on even her father's nerves."

"Gregory, I would say nothing on that subject. She is your daughter," Rosanna said.

"I appreciate that, my darling, and that is why

145

we are so well suited, each concerned by the needs and feelings of the other. And as I said, you need not worry about Lucy—"

"There is something else," Rosanna interrupted, wishing he were not so fond of talking.

"Say no more," the Count continued. "I know what you wish to discuss. Charles Cavanaugh, is it not?"

Rosanna felt her heart skip within her. "How did you know?" she asked.

"It was Lucy who first mentioned his name to me, and it was her meddlesome nature that led me to send her away. I had a talk with Sir Cavanaugh and he did confirm that there was nothing more than familial affection in his heart. He offered me sorely needed encouragement to pursue our plan. You see, I am not the cocksure *homme-du-monde* you thought me," he confessed.

"Gregory, I do not know what to say," Rosanna answered, as her breathing returned to its usual calm pace. She wanted so badly to tell him that it was far more than familial affection on her part, amour tender enough to cause her to put aside this marriage scheme. Even if the love was not returned, she could not ignore it nor even replace it with another kind for Lord Waltham.

"Rosanna, there is nothing that needs to be said. The matter is concluded and we need never broach it again," he promised. "Sir Cavanaugh explained it most clearly to me and I could understand, upon hearing the brotherly affection for you in his voice, how my daughter might have misunderstood his kindhearted address. But they are both gone from our lives, Charles Cavanaugh and Lucy, both . . . until the wedding."

"Will he be at the wedding?"

"If your father and his are such close acquaintances, I assume his presence," Gregory Waltham said as he drew his timepiece from within his breast-pocket. "I must leave you, dearest. I must be in my chambers early on the morrow." He kissed her hand. "I will leave you here in the garden and take with me a most beauteous picture."

His poetic adieu had little effect on the young lady, save that he left her sadly sorry she had not been allowed to say more. Perhaps she would have better luck the next afternoon; sit him down in the drawing room and open her heart . . .

When Rosanna was blessed with the comfort of her own bed that night, she was in a worse quandry than before, uncertain of her future with Charles and Lord Waltham, not having been able to make her feelings known to either one, stymied at every turn, thwarted at every path. She could only hope the morrow would bring tranquility. With that wish she fell asleep, her exasperated emotions giving over to slumber.

"You are a difficult man to locate, Sir Cavanaugh," Lord Playmore said, standing in the Oak Room at Peppernell's.

"Perhaps it is simply that I make myself available only to those I wish to see," Sir Charles answered.

"Then I must take it as a compliment that I see you," Lord Playmore would not be snubbed.

"You are a clever man, Baronet," the future Earl answered. "What assistance can I offer you?"

"I have a most personal matter to discuss with you. Might we find more private quarters?" Lord Playmore asked.

"If you insist," Charles answered, fully aware

147

that he would not be rid of the man until he heard what he had come to say.

When they were alone, in an alcove of the adjoining Grill Room, Sir Cavanaugh prefaced their discussion. "I must tell you that if this pertains to Lady Shelton I will have none of it."

"It does, and you will have to listen for I gave the dear lady my word I would speak with you—"

"And you have succeeded so I shan't make you a liar," Sir Cavanaugh said and began to leave the room. Lord Playmore's reflexes were swifter than the other man thought. A firm hand went out to stop his path. "I beg your pardon, Sir—"

But it was Lord Playmore who cut him off this time. "You may not think highly of me, Sir Cavanaugh, but I have enough self-respect to keep promises I make to those of her gender, to carry them through. . . . Does it not matter that Rosanna Shelton is in love with you?" he asked, paying careful attention to the expression on the other man's face, but it did not change. "Do you care not that you break her heart?"

"I do not understand how Rosanna might have asked you, a known intimate of hers, to intervene on her behalf," he said, the color in his cheeks, the edges of his Irish temper, now flaring.

"Lady Shelton did not ask. I offered, begged, in fact, to have this chance to remedy the confusion I created in your mind, the notion that she succumbed to me, when I pursued her shamelessly and all to no avail."

"I find that increasingly difficult to believe as Rosanna has shown me she will encourage any man who crosses her path," Charles Cavanaugh stated.

"You cannot believe that. If you are making reference to Gregory Waltham, you must know that

148

Rosanna met him long before she knew you and he could not have been put asunder as quickly as she would have liked, but she endeavors to do that now," the Baronet said.

"Your words mean nothing to me," Sir Cavanaugh insisted.

"Then you must read *her* words and then decide," the Baronet said and handed him the letter.

Sir Cavanaugh took the missive readily, tore it into four and let the pieces fall. "You may tell Lady Shelton what I have done with her note."

"Can't I give her any encouragement at all?"

"No, none. So there you are. I told you there was nothing to be done about this matter," Charles answered and watched the Baronet bow from the waist and leave the room. He picked up the torn letter from the floor and put the scraps inside his coat pocket. He would not read it today, but perhaps next week, when his heart had begun to mend and forget her cruelty then he would read it and find some appeasement.

Charles Cavanaugh was a stubborn-willed man, through no fault of his own, but a trait he had inherited from his native land. It made him do things he did not often wish to do such as denying himself the pleasure of Rosanna's company because he was too intemperate to forgive her mistake or let it pass.

Lord Playmore did not relish the task he had before him, the message he had to relay to Lady Shelton. But he knew it was best to get it done as soon as possible, before she had the time to build any false hopes or sink deeper into despair. He found Rosanna much as he had the previous day, wandering aimlessly about the drawing room, staring out

149

onto the patio, standing by the fireplace and running her hand along the cold marble, crossing to the window seat to gaze distractedly on Curzon Street.

"Lady Shelton," he called softly.

"Lord Playmore, have you seen him?" she asked, coming alive.

"I have," he answered in a low voice that told her all she needed to know. "I am sorry."

"He would not even read it, would he?"

"But I did leave it with him," Playmore answered, thinking it sufficient.

"He has, no doubt, burned it," Rosanna said bitterly.

"You must allow time to heal his hurt pride, he feels deceived, a horrid blow to a man as strong-willed as he."

"As because he is so strong-willed, he will never forgive me," Rosanna said. "I must stop believing that his love for me should forgive me anything."

"What will you do now?" the Baronet asked.

"I suspect, Lord Playmore, that I shall do rightly by at least one man. Count Waltham. I must live up to my word and follow through with our plans."

"Do you mean to marry him, though you do not love him?"

"I gave him my word."

Chapter Eleven

The first day of June was without a doubt one of the rainiest London had seen in a month. Was it an omen? Rosanna wondered, as the downstairs servants moved all the floral arrangements indoors from the patio before they were ruined. The reception would have to be held in the drawing room of the Shelton house.

"The garland of white roses can be used around the bannister," Lady Simpson directed. "The two large vases on either side of the mantle will accommodate the mums," she continued, standing in her dressing gown, her hair still in wrappers.

Round tables were placed in front of the now closed patio doors and reset with dry linen.

"We will have to open the dining apartment as well," the nervous grandmother went on. "There is nary enough room in here to accomodate the guests!"

"Have you any suggestion?" Lord Shelton asked as he helped one of the servants with the pianoforte that had been moved outdoors and in again in the space of an hour, so swiftly and unexpectedly had the rains come.

"No, Father," Rosanna said with indifference. Already in her wedding gown, she sat silently in an armchair. "I leave it to your able jugdment."

"Rosanna, it is not too late to call an end to this marriage charade," her father said softly.

"Why should I do that?" she asked innocently.

"Because a smile has not appeared on your face for weeks, and today, the day of your wedding, you are more sullen, if that is possible," he told her.

"I am . . . pensive. Nothing more. I am thinking about how I am to leave this house today, kiss my family and begin a new life," she answered, looking at the rivulets of water streaming down the bay window.

"Child, you have been talking of nothing else since you were a girl of sixteen. I should think you would have no more to ponder on that subject," Lord Shelton said.

"Talking of it and putting the plan into effect, they are two different things."

"I suppose," her father agreed, but could not find it in his heart to believe that was all that concerned his offspring.

"You must finish dressing," Rosanna said, rising to adjust her father's ascot. "We should not be late," she said. "You have yet to put on your morning jacket."

"Cast a glance at your grandmother," he suggested, but Lady Simpson had slipped from the room before either could hasten her out. "And you, Rosanna, will you not dress your visage as befits a bride?"

"Father?"

"Your smile, dear girl," he said, knowing full well not even that could put one on his own face. He could not reconcile himself to the fact that Charles Cavanaugh had been lost to them. He knew, through Christina Chattering, that they had had even the Baronet's assistance. What could have squashed the plans? He looked about his drawing room, watching all the preparations being made for a wedding no one in the house cared a whit about.

"I will consent to try," Rosanna said and excused herself. Perhaps a hint of rouge would add warmth to her complexion. She would ask Betty's assistance; her own hands were as cold as ice.

The Earl was left to ponder his daughter's future. Would it be as bleak as the morn? he asked himself.

"She still has time to change her mind, Arthur," Lady Simpson said, adjusting the strand of pearls she wore over the lace gown, the color of juniper berries.

"There is very little time left, Dorothy. I think the hand is over and we have lost," he said sadly.

She placed a comforting hand on his shoulder and they thought silently of Rosanna, of the years of her childhood, her early womanhood. "There is still time," she repeated, clinging to that hope, trying to heed her own words of advice: "Do not despair."

"Whatever Rosanna decides, we must go along with her," he said reluctantly.

When the bride descended, both parent and grandparent could not keep from looking upon her with pride in their eyes. Never was she more beautiful, those eyes more startling, than against her rosied complexion and the whiteness of her lace veil and cap.

"You present a vision that every father dreams of from the moment his daughter is born," the Earl said. "You are lovely."

"Thank you, Father," she said and hugged him tightly. "Is it time?" she asked, in a voice more reminiscent of the former Queen Anne (that Boleyn woman, as much of England still thought her) as she was about to meet the most ablest swordsman of all Christendom.

"The carriage is ready," Alcott announced.

"Shall we go?" she asked, turning to take her grandmother's hand.

The chapel was as beautifully decorated as the Shelton drawing room, fragrant with garlands of roses and lilies strung about each pew. The aisle was covered with a white carpet, unrolled only as the bride arrived and goodly so, for there were at least a hundred pairs of muddied shoes that had preceeded Rosanna.

The rain did not subside for even the half-hour it took the carriage to reach the church. The guests spoke noisily among themselves until word of Rosanna's presence was circulated.

Lady Simpson gave her granddaughter a final kiss in the vestibule and went to claim her seat.

Reverent McFarland greeted Rosanna and her father, and offered a few words of inspiration before he joined the groom at the alter.

Rosanna lowered the veil over her face and, clutching them in trembling hands, took her bouquet of white roses and lilies from her father.

As the music began, she had a most unsteady feeling in her limbs, caused by the tightening in her stomach. She knew, as though she were looking clear through a crystal ball, that she was making a tragic mistake, and yet her body moved forward with the rhythm of the music.

The Reverend, whom she had known since her birth, sounded like a stranger to her ears as he asked her father to give her hands to the groom. Her hands trembled so much that her bouquet dropped to the floor. Her heart leapt into her throat.

As Count Waltham knelt to retrieve it, as Father McFarland began to address the congregation, Rosanna turned to look at the great venue of friends and family who had gathered to share this day with her. In the fast blink of an eye, she saw Lucy James and her husband, Christina Chattering and Mr. Pericles, Lord and Lady Wolverton, Miss Beaufort—the faces began swimming one into the next as her eyes quickly traveled back further and further, row after row until she caught sight of the doorway leading to the lane.

She saw Charles Cavanaugh standing in front of the doors and she blinked, doubting her own eyes. But when they opened again, he was gone. Was he there at all? Where did he go? Suddenly she realized that these were the only questions she wanted to answer that day, certainly none that called for those two words . . . .

Rosanna faced Lord Waltham. He held out her bouquet to her. The Reverend stopped, waiting for her to take the flowers before he went on. But Rosanna lifted her skirts after winding the train of her veil about her wrist and ran down the length of the aisle to her freedom.

Charles Cavanaugh was nowhere in sight when she reached the street, and she stood transfixed for a moment before realizing that someone would come after her at any second. She jumped inside her awaiting carriage and rapped on the partition to catch the attention of the dozing attendant.

Rosanna did not realize that someone was indeed at her heels and had climbed aboard the carriage.

"Lord Playmore! What a start you gave me! But how did you escape so quickly?" Rosanna asked.

The Baronet ignored her for a moment, giving hasty directions to the groom, who had quickly seized the reins of his horses with his mistress's alarming knock.

"This is not another attempt at seduction, I hope," Rosanna said, unable to resist the humor of the situation.

"An attempt at survival, dear lady—yours! No less than a hundred people will be at your heels in only the time it takes for a stampede to gather itself together," he assured her.

Rosanna turned around to see if she had been followed by any others. The carriage had already begun to move.

"How did you get away?" Rosanna asked.

"Indirectly, I suspect—you've your father to thank. Lord Waltham was to take after you in a shot, but your father restrained him, insisting you would return as soon as you collected your thoughts, I think he said. I believe the Earl was affording you extra seconds for your 'get away'—is that not what the Americans call it?"

"Are you likening me to those rebels?" Rosanna asked, laughing.

"You can be likened to no one, dear Lady Shelton. Perhaps that is the reason every man in London seeks to kneel upon your doorstep," Lord Playmore vowed.

156

"Dear friend, I know you seek to lighten my spirit, but even your solicitous words of flattery fall on unreceptive ears. I am afraid, Lord Playmore," Rosanna confessed. "What a mess I have made, and in front of everyone."

"You need time as your ally, Lady Shelton. You will stay at my home until night falls and we shall send round a dispatch to your father. He will fetch you as soon as Lord Waltham beats his retreat," he promised.

"I have been too stunned by my own actions to thank you for helping me. If you did not instruct the groom to take us to Brompton Court, I don't know what would have become of me. I could not return home—they would have followed me there first," she sighed.

"I will assure you safety in my library. Only the parlor is visible from the street. No one shall walk by to espy you within," he promised.

Rosanna took his hand and was silent until she was well esconsed in that wood-paneled room.

"Can I have my housekeeper fix you a cup of tea to soothe you?" The Baronet asked, not sure of how to treat her. He laughed at his confusion; were she here on any other reason, he thought to himself, he would know well how to tend to her.

"Tea would be nice," Rosanna said, "I, too, am not familiar with what one serves an escaped bride in lieu of champagne."

Rosanna was silent again, but soon after the tea arrived a thought crossed her mind. As innocently as a child placing a piece in a puzzle, she asked, "Have I done the right thing?"

"Do you love Waltham?" her host asked.

She shook her head vehemently.

"Then you have done correctly."

"He will never forgive me ... I will never be able to hold my head high again. And the worst of it is the gossip my father will have to hear," Rosanna said.

"I can see something else troubles you," the Baronet said. "Would it help to share it?"

"I wanted a house of my own ... an understanding husband, or so I thought. But what I really want is ... the love of Charles Cavanaugh, but he won't even talk to me." As she thought back to the boldness of her quitting the church, of the many hours of deliberation that had led her to that decision, of the anguish she felt at the thought of how this must be hurting Lord Waltham, she broke into sobs and fell into Lord Playmore's arms, surprising him in such a way that an observer would think he had never before held a lady so close to his breast!

"Rosanna, I will marry you!" he proclaimed. "And I will endeavor to make you forget Waltham and Cavanaugh for each is a scoundrel! Worse, I think! For making you so miserable," he added.

"What a noble gesture, Lord Playmore. But I could not allow it. "You must find yourself a bride who will love you, though I do not think you would be happy with marriage's limitations. You thrive on life's intrigues and marriage offers little enough of that, I think."

"And what of you, dear one, do you thrive on love letters and abandoned altars? Could we not together find such intrigue within marriage?"

"There is much appreciation for all you have done for me today, most of all for this charming offer of marriage. But it would not be fair of me to accept. The mystery you find in our friendship would dissipate in the space of a honeymoon, and I would not have that for all the world," Rosanna

158

explained, thinking him the dearest man in all the world.

"If you refuse me, I must think of another way to make you happy again."

"All that I ask of is a solitary hour or two in this fine room ... until I can return home and begin to explain what I have done. If you could send Father a note saying that all is well, I would return home through the darkness of the kitchen and climb the backstairs if Waltham has not quit the house. To fall asleep in my bed," Rosanna said, longing for its soft comfort.

"That is easily arranged," her host said, disappointed that there was no other magical feat he could be prevailed upon to perform.

"The turnabout in your character, your constant friendship, is more miraculous than anything the heavens could divine," Rosanna said. "Now you must allow me to freshen your tea for I've no doubt I made it intolerably salty with my tears, crying over you in such a fashion."

Lord Playmore complied with Rosanna's request for solitude and took his teacup into the parlor. He looked out from the window, onto Brompton Court proper to assure himself that they had not been followed. He returned to the library, wishing just to tell her of her continued safety. But he stood silently in the doorway, thinking of how charming she looked, a young lady in her wedding gown, her face streaked with tears, her veil crumpled on the floor, her hands caught in the demi-gloved sleeves, wrestling to butter a scone. Amusing, yet charming all the same. He wished he could have this portrait, but was content to carry this picture with him in his mind.

Rosanna toasted herself with her teacup unaware that her friend watched. She replaced it in its saucer and rested her head against the sofa cushion. All the anxiety of the previous night and that short morning conspired together, and she fell promptly to sleep. Lord Playmore ventured to her side only to cover her with a modest wool throw and left her to rest.

His housekeeper was waiting for him in the parlor.

"You've a visitor, Lordship. One Lady Chattering. Shall I show her up?"

"Indeed," Lord Playmore insisted, smacking his lips guiltily. "Indeed," he repeated impatiently, wondering what she could want.

The grin on his face told that he had not mended his ways in the least, save where Lady Shelton was concerned. He thought of Christina Chattering as he did all other women, a pigeon come to rest in his nest. That she was more a peacock with that fiery red hair and those sapphire eyes did not seem to bother him in the least, now that he was over his infatuation with her *amie*.

"We meet twice in a morning; I am most fortunate," he greeted her as she entered his parlor. "I am honored, too, that you seek me out in my own apartment."

"Lord Playmore, do not flatter yourself," she cautioned, but with a playful look in her eyes. "You know why I am here—to see Rosanna."

"How did you divine that she was here?" he asked, not confirming or denying the assumption.

"She has made no secret of your recent friendship," Lady Chattering told him, and then added, "and I was not unaware of the hasty retreat you made from the church, yet you were nowhere to be found in the lane."

"I can only hope that the jilted groom is not half so astute, dear guest," he said and offered her repose on his sofa.

"Thank you," Christina said, "To alleviate your fears, I can say that no one else suspects—oh, perhaps Lord Shelton, but he is hardly one to tell the Count where he might pick up the scent," she said, alluding to that fateful day of the hunt at the Wolverton estate.

"Lady Chattering, your remarks afford me much comfort. I should not know what to do if the Count appeared, though I am certain your feminine wiles could prove distracting for a time," he said flatteringly.

"Baronet, you toy with me as always, through you know I find you charming," she confessed bluntly. Finding herself alone with him and in such close quarters caused her to act in so alien a fashion.

"Would you prefer drama, dear lady?" he asked, willing to give her all the elan she desired.

"It would make the game more intriguing," she said.

"Then we must plan a secret rendezvous in the the country to seal our friendship," he proposed, drawing her hand into his.

"Lord Playmore!" she protested mildly as she thought most befitted a woman who had just, without thinking, offered herself so freely.

"Do you not find that scheme pleasant?" he asked, bringing her hand to his lips.

"Tis divine inspiration," she boldly admitted. "But now you must tell me about Rosanna," she said, the truer purpose of her visit coming back into her head—thankfully, she thought, for heaven only knew what further liberties could be taken!

"Your friend rests comfortably in the library—I am afraid we must leave her alone for a time. I did all I could to rescue her from her funk. I believe a few days' time might go farther than even my marriage proposal," the Baronet said.

"Your proposal?" she asked shocked.

"She rejected me, naturally," he said, not the least bit dejected.

"'Tis a relief," Lady Chattering muttered under her breath, unaware that the Baronet felt precisely the same.

"But do tell me, was there much frenzy when you left the church?"

"You could not imagine the half of it—a scene unequalled in any opera. Lord Waltham, I thought, was about to have a seizure of the heart. His sister, the wretch, began howling in so wolf-like a fashion one could have no doubt wherein she derived her name. Her husband, it must be said, was calm, and his niece and stepdaughter could nary refrain for a tizzy of laughter, thinking of the delight to be derived from doing the same to those hams they call beaux. Lord Shelton near fainted dead away—from relief, I suspect, while dear Lady Dorothy blotted her forehead with a hankerchief, saying to herself, 'still time, still time.' She appeared to recover sufficiently to silence their friends and beg their forgiveness for having put them to such trouble this day.

"It was not so much that Rosanna called a halt to the proceedings, but that she disappeared in so frightful a fashion. Lord Waltham was beside himself, insisting that his man of business would consult the Shelton man of business this very noon! To appease the guests, Lord Shelton invited them all to his home to consume the elaborate buffet prepared

162

for the celebration—odd to have the only bride and groom atop the wedding cake!

"As soon as I was satisfied that Rosanna had not slipped upstairs unnoticed, I determined to proceed here to seek her out."

"I am sorry to have missed such a gala—tell me, did Lord Shelton have the orchestra play as well?"

"There was little enough room within the house—every last guest at the church was present, each hoping to find out a morsel of gossip, no doubt. But before the musicians were dismissed, they did stand upon the stairs and offer *God Save The King*," Lady Chattering said. "It was most unique," she added generously. "I am only glad Rosanna was not there to witness it."

"Indeed," Lord Playmore said, "though I can well understand the Earl's good spirits."

"They would be further improved if I could bring him word that Rosanna is well," Lady Chattering said, trying once again to see her friend.

"I was about to pen him a letter at her request," Lord Playmore said. "She wishes to wait until dark to return home, when the chances of her being seen are greatly diminished. She is feeling a touch of humiliation, I'm afraid."

"There is no reason for it. Her family loves her as ever and her true friends are at her side. I, for one, have had enough of Lady Wolverton and her set, and care not a whit after their opinions. Rosanna, too, has no doubt realized that cultivating that type of acquaintance does not afford one any greater spirit or character," Lady Chattering said.

"There is only one person Rosanna cares after now. Charles Cavanaugh."

"Is she still convinced there is no hope?"

"And rightly so. I have spoken to him myself," Lord Playmore said. "I saw the fury in his eyes—he is not the kind of man who forgives or forgets quickly. His Irish blood."

"No doubt, but how foolish that two who could love so deeply should never get the chance because of excessive pride. There must be some way to unite them, to bring Charles to his senses and have them admit their feelings for each other," Christina said.

"But how? Unless we are to set the example," he turned the conversation around to his own purposes.

"What did you have in mind?" Lady Chattering asked in a coquettish voice.

"An excursion to Bognor Regis would please you?" he suggested.

"It should be quite pleasant this time of year," Christina agreed. "I would not be at all adverse to the adventure."

"Then Bognor Regis it shall be," he concluded.

"I will wait to hear more definite plans from you," she said, wholly aroused by this turn of events.

"Perhaps during our excursion we shall be prompted by an idea to unite Rosanna and Charles," he said, though at that very moment he was most concerned with how he might unite his arms around Lady Chattering's slender waist.

Chapter Twelve

"Rosanna, you cannot barricade yourself in your room in the hope that you might avoid Lord Waltham for the rest of your life," the Earl pleaded with her. "He knows that you have not deserted our country and he has called here every morning for the past week. You must come out, daughter, if for your own good health, to stroll about the garden.

"If not for your good health, then our peace of mind," Lady Simpson added as she stood beside her son-in-law.

If they had been worried about Rosanna before the wedding, their concern had only increased since the moment she had quit the church.

Rosanna's door opened this time and she presented herself in a dressing gown of rose satin that, her relations thought, hung much too loosely on her slender frame. Her hair was pulled back in a tight

165

bun; she had not let Betty care for it since the day of the wedding. Her skin was more pale than usual, and yet, it made her appear more romantic and fairy-like.

Lord Shelton opened his arms to hold her, so relieved was he that she had finally agreed to leave her chamber.

"Father," Rosanna sobbed as she embraced him. "You were so right... about everything. What a dreadful mistake I have made ..."

"Rosanna, you were able to keep yourself from making the most tragic error of all—marrying the Count. Therefore you have no reason to cry. You should be overjoyed as I am," he said, hoping to comfort her.

"I love you, Father," Rosanna said, slowly trying to regain her composure.

"And I love you, daughter. But it pains me to see you so heartbroken. How can I be of assistance?" he asked.

"There is nothing to be done... I have lost Charles ..." she said between sobs.

"Can nothing be done?" her grandmother asked.

"No. It is too late. Only your love and comfort will afford any relief for my anguish," Rosanna said.

"You have that," Lady Simpson said.

"There is only one other obstacle before us," her father said. "I hoped to put it off, but it will plague us until we see to its resolution. Lord Waltham," he spoke the name ominously.

"What am I to say to him, Father? Do I apologize? What if he asks to set another plan for a wedding?"

"Lord Waltham finally understands you have had a change of heart. It was all our man of business could do to keep him from bringing a formal charge of breech of promise against us at first. But he is more reasonable now. He seeks to mend his bruised reputation, Rosanna, and to understand why you cast him aside so sharply. That is all he seeks to hear from you," her father explained, demonstrating his compassion for the man.

"I can quite imagine the Count's horror. Perhaps I had better change to more suitable attire if you expect him shortly," Rosanna said.

"We will wait for you below," he added thoughtfully, as he released her slowly from his grasp.

Lord Waltham and his daughter Lucy arrived well before Rosanna descended. Lady Simpson invited Mrs. James into the garden, ostensibly to show her the flowers.

"I did not think we would succeed," Lady Simpson confessed. "Of course, I would have rather it had not been in so public a way . . ."

"Though my father suffered greatly that day, I believe it was worth it. He was fit to be tied, even blamed it on me—the work of a half decanter of brandy. My Aunt Irva did not offer him the greatest solace either," she added. "But I think now all begin to forget the embarrassment."

Lady Simpson was too considerate a woman to express the same candor in regard to the Shelton family's opinion of the Wolvertons. She simply told Lucy she was glad their families were dis-united with little disaccord. When Rosanna descended, the two women were joined by Lord Shelton who had left his daughter in the drawing room with her former fiancé.

At first, there was much agitation in that room

for neither Rosanna nor Gregory Waltham spoke. And when one did, the other began as well. They both laughed, dissolving much of the anger that had involuntarily sprung from each to the other.

"Please, Rosanna, go ahead," the Count insisted.

"I wish to tell you how deeply sorry I am for the embarrassment I have caused you and your family. If I had thought for even one moment before I quit the church that I would not proceed with the marriage, I would have told you so. It was the only path I saw to take, dear Lord Waltham," she confessed.

"Such formality does not become two friends," he said to her. "Pray tell me, was it something I did to offend you?"

"No, never, Gregory. And I wished to marry you because of all your kindness and thoughtful intentions. It was only when I realized that keeping my promise would make us both unhappy after a time that I knew I could not go ahead with the plan. I could not bear the thought of giving you a lifetime of unhappiness—it seemed as though the discomfort of our wedding day would quickly pass, and was far less distasteful medicine than the daily reminder of a sour marriage," Rosanna said, her voice steady and calm though filled with tenderness.

"Rosanna, are you in love with another?"

"Yes," she answered with candor.

"Sir Cavanaugh?" he asked.

"Yes, but that is my penance," she said. "By not telling him of our engagement from the first, I hurt him as well and have lost him forever."

"A few days ago I would have said that you have gotten your just desserts, but now, seeing you o saddened, I find only sympathy for you in my heart," he said kindly. "Can there be no hope?"

"None," she said. "He did refuse any explanation of our friendship before our wedding day ... I will never have even the opportunity to tell him I am sorry. But that signifies little—if he does not love me, he will surely not deign to forgive me."

"My daughter Lucy had me so convinced of his affection for you that I was persuaded to sound him out on the subject. But he would have denied it under any circumstances—a man would not admit to loving the fiancé of another. His recent knowledge of our relationship would explain his particularly cold attitude that day—and that tells me that he does love you. I am surprised that did not seem more obvious to me at the time. I suppose it did, and that I tried to ignore it. My vanity would not permit me to accept as young and able a contestant for your affections. But if there is no hope for you and Sir Cavanaugh—"

"Lord Waltham, my heart will never be free of him," Rosanna answered before he could finish. "Marriage to another would be cheating both bride and groom."

"I understand," Lord Waltham said and asked if there was any way to assist her.

"Being completely removed from our usual circle of acquaintances has helped ease my heart," she said.

"And I will not tax you any longer," he assured her, reluctant just the same to quit her side. "I think we both know what happened; with time's help, we shall put it aside."

"You will always be someone very dear to me," she told him.

169

"That knowledge makes an old man's folly easier to live with," he said and took her hand one last time. "Until next we meet."

He reclaimed his daughter and left Rosanna as she wished, in the bosom of her family.

Rosanna joined her father and grandmother in the garden, seating herself on the white wrought iron bench, her face tilted towards the comforting sun.

But the Sheltons were not unvisited for long. Lady Chattering soon presented herself in the drawing room with her constant companion, Mr. Gaylord Pericles.

Lord Shelton greeted them alone.

"Good day, dear Christina," he said warmly, still surprising her with his new dialogue.

"Does your improved spirit indicate that Rosanna has join our good ranks anew?" she asked, removing her feathered bonnet.

"Yes, yes. She has even consented to speak to the Count, though she will have nothing more to do with that clan," he said happily. "Except Mr. Pericles, certainly," he added, remembering the man's distant attachment to the Wolverton family.

"I have renounced them as well," Christina said frankly.

"And I am not so close a relation as to feel slighted, nor as to be counted as a Wolverton," Mr. Pericles added, easing the mood.

"Besides all that," Christina said, "I am working on a scheme to reunite the two lovers."

"Might I be of some assistance?" Lord Shelton volunteered. "Anything at all!"

"No, it is too soon for your part, but perhaps in a few days," she said, "I will let you know when your assistance is needed."

While they spoke, Lady Simpson sought to comfort her granddaughter. "So your child will have a few more sweaters before it is born," she said smiling. "There have been worse tragedies."

Rosanna sat silently.

"Is your love for him causing so much pain?" Dorothy asked.

"It is difficult to love someone knowing that your feelings will always go unanswered."

"Always is a very long time," her grandmother told her. "Perhaps it will take less for Charles Cavanaugh to realize it is a mistake to relinquish your love so easily. Remember that it has only been a few weeks—and he may not even know that you and Lord Waltham are not married."

"I am sure he knows, having had to pay quite a few debts on that score," she said, alluding to the wagers that has been placed in her honor.

"What do you mean?"

"It is not important," Rosanna said. "Very little seems to matter these days."

Rosanna fell sullen again until her friends appeared in the garden.

"Rosanna, how is it that we have not seen you all week?" Christina asked with mock reproach.

"I have seen no one, though many have called, Christina. You were not among them—nor Lord Playmore," Rosanna said, without attaching any significance to that fact.

Christina could not yet tell Rosanna the reason for her absence, and had insisted that Lord Playmore remain silent as well. She was not entirely sure of what her friend's reaction would be and did not wish to cause her any further distress.

"I cannot account for Lord Playmore," Christina said awkwardly.

"I do not expect you to. I mention it only because I find it odd. I have come to depend on him for lifting my spirits," Rosanna explained. "I see him in so different a light."

"You do?" Christina asked, encouraged.

"Even Father approves of his friendship. We should not judge so harshly and quickly in the future. I am glad to have all my friends close by. How have you been, Mr. Pericles?"

"I have been absent from London for a time, and was distressed to learn that you are saddened," he said, though his thoughtfullness divulged his ever present propensity for gossip.

"It will pass," Rosanna said, thanking him for his concern. "Time is the perfect antidote for love sickness."

"If only we could go round to the chemist for one more hasty remedy. Perhaps a *vacances* is in order," she suggested. "The seashore would provide a pleasant change from London—nothing so far nor as primitive as France nor Spain, but a short jaunt. We do not have to leave the motherland."

"Indeed not," interjected Lord Shelton, with renewed fatherly anxiety.

Alcott entered the garden to announce the arrival of Lord Playmore, bring a smile to Rosanna's face and prompting an "Oh goodness!" from her best friend.

"There, there," Mr. Pericles said to Christina in a whisper. "He won't bite you here."

"How marvelous to see you and Christina both," Rosanna said, as the Baronet appeared.

"Lady Chattering is here now?" Lord Playmore asked.

"Yes, along with Mr. Pericles," Rosanna answered.

172

"Ah! Mr. Pericles! How are you?" The Baronet asked though he had never taken the slightest interest in the man. "And Lady Chattering—how long has it been? Since the wedding?"

"If I did not know you both better, I would swear you were meeting for the first time when all the world knows you are intimate!" Rosanna exclaimed.

"What?" Christina begged her pardon.

"What!" Lord Playmore echoed.

"Well, you act as though you have never before seen each other—as though by demons possessed," Rosanna explained.

"Perhaps you are overwrought," Christina suggested. "I greet Playmore no differently than always—I mean on those occasions when we meet—I mean by accident, of course," she stumbled guiltily.

"We are all concerned after you," the Baronet tried to smooth over the conversation.

"But you can see that I am in fine spirits," Rosanna said, feigning a great smile.

"If we could only believe it," Lord Playmore said.

"You will, dear friends. A bit more private contemplation and I will bloom again, as vibrant as ever. It is only that I am still so tired from the whole affair," she explained.

"Then I will take my leave," the Baronet suggested.

"But I was going to leave now," Christina interrupted.

"You are both free to use the front door at the same time," Rosanna said. 'Curzon Street will accommodate your leaving together."

"Together?" Christina and the Baronet asked almost in unison.

"But you are a strange pair today," Rosanna said and led the way through the drawing room. "For myself, I will return to my chamber to finish the book of poems I have begun." She kissed her friends and left them in the foyer.

The concerned expression returned to the Earl's face upon his daughter's departure.

Christina took his hand and said, "If I persuaded Lord Chattering to marry me, I will have little trouble with Sir Cavanaugh and your daughter—they have the advantage of being in love."

"Her fate and mine rests with you then," the Earl said ominously, "though I see no easy solution in the offing."

"Perhaps Lord Playmore and Christina will pool their talents," Mr. Pericles said naughtily, prompting his friend to remind herself to slap his hand at the earliest convenience.

"Perhaps," Lord Shelton answered, unaware of the intrigue in front of his nose. He wished them a safe journey and joined his mother-in-law on the sofa in silent reflection.

"How awkward!" Christina said as the trio reached the lane.

"Well, how was I to know that you would choose this morning, the first since our return, to visit our friend?" the Baronet asked.

"I can't say why the two of you fuss so. I don't think Rosanna would object to your ... liaison," Mr. Pericles said.

"You mean our friendship," she hastened to correct him. "But it is still only a year that poor Egbert has been lost to us all. I should not wish to incur the attention of every rake and gossip in town," she added, still sensible to her tenuous position in society.

174

She and the Baronet prepared to part company at the carriage house.

"Perhaps we can meet later at Mr. Pericles'," the Baronet suggested.

"I wish you would find another guardian for your tête-à-têtes, now that you are returned," Mr. Pericles said. "In your presence, I find a chill in the night air."

"But the evenings were so warm," Christina reminisced. "Can we take another sojourn to Bognor Regis soon?" she asked though they were so recently returned.

"You might take Rosanna with you this time, so that I would not have to concoct any tales about being with the Prince," Gaylord said, undesirous of playing chaperone with these two again.

"Take Rosanna?" Playmore questioned.

"She is all alone in this house, no young people to keep her company—she could do with the change," Gaylord continued, hoping to talk them into it. As long as he remained the only one privy to this new romance, his own evening plans would be curtailed out of loyalty to his friend Christina.

"Would you join us and make it a foursome?" Christina asked.

"Rosanna would enjoy Charles Cavanaugh far more," Mr. Pericles said.

"How am I to get Charles Cavanaugh in a carriage with Rosanna—" she began to denounce his plan when an idea came to her mind and she took her full attention to contemplate its fruition.

"What is it, Christina?" the Baronet asked. "Are you unwell?" he worried that she might swoon from the June heat.

"Christina, answer us," Mr. Pericles implored.

"I have just divined the perfect way to reunite the lovers," Christina announced.

"Will you keep us in suspense until the next frost?" Gaylord Pericles asked anxiously.

"I can't tell you yet. But we three shall meet this evening and I will furnish you with all the details," she promised. "Now let us adjourn for I have much to arrange. Lord Playmore, would you have your groom take Mr. Pericles home?"

"Of course," the Baronet said and the two men watched dumbfounded as Christina boarded her carriage and disappeared down the lane.

"Whatever could that scatterbrained mind be plotting?" Mr. Pericles asked and turned to exchange a most quizzical expression with the Baronet.

Chapter Thirteen

"Christina, I would be terrible company for you, though it is very kind of you to ask," Rosanna said. "Why would you want me in your party, when I am in so dreadful a temper?" she asked, clutching her lace handkerchief.

"Rosanna, mourning does not suit you. You cannot linger on the vine as Sir Cavanaugh thrives in every matchmaking mama's parlor. And the excursion is planned for the sole purpose of lifting your mood, though I must confess escaping this early heat would be reward enough for the journey," her friend explained, hoping to persuade her.

"Has he begun a courtship?" Rosanna asked, desperately clutching her bosom.

"Who?" Christina asked.

"Sir Cavanaugh, of course!" her friend snapped.

"Are you still upon that ancient subject? Really

Rosanna, I cannot believe you . . . I do not know anything of the kind, but I can assure you that he is not sitting at home bemoaning the fact that he almost lost you to another!"

"Christina, forgive me my obsession. It shall not continue indefinitely. But I think that if I cry long enough, the pain will dissipate sooner and I shall be like before."

"I disagree, Rosanna, for if you cry every day, you shall get quite used to the consolation of patient friends and will not soon give it up," Lady Chattering reasoned. "Soon you will take absolute pleasure in it and forget what real pleasure is. Now I must insist that you accompany me. Perhaps I will ask Lord Playmore and Mr. Pericles to join us—"

"Then I will most definitely decline, for I shall be miserable company for them and could not bear it," Rosanna insisted.

"Very well," Christina acquiesced before her plot was ruined. "You and I will go alone and reside with my Aunt Vilna."

"I don't know . . ." Rosanna hesitated.

"Why don't you ask your grandmother's sage opinion," Christina suggested, already cognizant of the dear Lady's thoughts on the matter.

Lady Simpson was familiarly bent over her knitting needles in her favored chair, listening to this exchange, saying nothing until she was asked.

"What do you think, Grandmother?"

"Granddaughter, I would not have you take this the wrong way, but you are a dreadful sight in the drawing room, that long face moping about all day and evening. If you must know, I spend as much time as I deem appropriate above for my heart breaks at the sight of you so thin and pale.

The seashore would at least put a hint of color in those cheeks. You must go with dear Christina. She has gone to extreme lengths to improve your condition; it is the least you can do," Lady Simpson said.

"Will you accompany me?" Rosanna asked.

"You do not need my company, nor a chaperone—we've learned that much from this experience. If it was only freedom you wanted, you ought to have asked . . . and months ago!"

"I must see what Father thinks," Rosanna said, procrastinating further still.

"Father would agree with any scheme that would get you out of doors again," her grandparent said with little hesitation.

"So you are all against me," Rosanna realized. "No doubt you've enlisted Alcott and Betty, too."

"If need be," Dorothy answered truthfully.

"Then I must accept," she told her pleased friend. "When is the grand expedition to take place?"

"If we are to reach Aunt Vilna's home before nightfall, we must leave early in the day. Six in the morning to be precise," Christina said.

"But that is still night! It would be a wonder for the horses to see the road before them," Roasnna cried. "What an unnatural hour to have to waken from one's slumber. Why, if I am to be properly coiffed and dressed, I shall have to rise at four! Christina—"

"Do not argue, Rosanna. You can sleep enroute" her friend promised. "And you needn't wonder after Aunt Vilna's impression of you upon our arrival. She knows well the length of the journey."

"If there was but a party the previous night, I need not have to ever go to sleep!"

"Rosanna, there are parties every night, you simply choose never to attend," her friend reminded her.

"When are we to put off?" Rosanna asked.

"In the morning, of course."

"Tomorrow? But that is hardly time to prepare—" Rosanna protested.

"Betty will start on your things at once. I'll see to it presently," Lady Simpson said and quit the room, stopping only to pat Christina's shoulder.

"I'll give her a list of clothes you'll need and come rouse you myself in the morning if you like," Christina offered.

"I've no doubt Betty can see to that, dear one," Rosanna said. "If I did not know better, I would think you all conspired to remove me from London!"

"We do, Rosanna," her friend confessed, avowing more than Rosanna realized.

"Thank you, Christina, for all your concern," Rosanna said, knowing that without this impetus she might have languished on Curzon Street indefinitely. "Until the morrow—if I can make you out in the darkness!"

"Indeed," Christina replied, not finding that comment, too on the mark, to be amusing.

There was no doubt in Lord Playmore's mind that Sir Cavanaugh would not consent to speak with him under any circumstances. He knew as he entered Peppernell's on that same morning that he would have to seek out one of Sir Cavanaugh's intimates or have no luck at all furthering his lady love's scheme.

He lingered outside the Oak Room before he dared peak through the open doorway to see if Sir Charles were inside. Indeed he was, reading a morning daily by the window. He was alone in the room and therefore, Lord Playmore reasoned, anyone who wished to join him would have to cross the Baronet's path first. He only hoped he recognized one of the other young gallant's from his visit to these quarters, far removed from his prefered haunts above, some weeks before.

When Mr. Robert Daniels appeared, the Baronet requested his company for a few moments in the Billiards Room where they might speak privately.

"What is this all about?" Mr. Daniels asked.

"It concerns your friend, Charles Cavanaugh, and his continued happiness on this earth," Lord Playmore said ominously.

"Is Charles in some sort of scrap?" his friend asked, paying careful attention to the Baronet.

"No—unless you consider trouble a broken heart."

"Ah ... it has to do with Lady Shelton then. You know of his grief?"

"Is it grief?" Lord Playmore wished to ascertain.

"There is not a man in his circle who does not know how he pines for the Lady," Mr. Daniels admitted.

"She would find these, sorely needed words for encouragement," he answered.

"But what have you to do with this? I have seen you speak to Bonnie Charlie once before—you left him in quite a state," Bob Daniels became more concerned.

"I seek only to reunite them," Lord Playmore explained. "I have a scheme. If you are the friend you claim to be and would like to see his heart mended, perhaps you would not be adverse to listening to what I have to say." He closed the door of the room they were now standing in.

When the Baronet reopened the door, some moments later, Mr. Daniels slapped him playfully on the back and said. "'Tis a rare plan indeed. You have my assistance in bringing it about. I will do just as you requested and hope for the best outcome. If there is to be a wedding in the offing, I'll see to it you stand beside Sir Cavanaugh. There are none I know who could have divined such inspiration, all in the name of glory love."

"Can it really be a June morn, Betty?" Rosanna asked, shivering in her nightshift. The wood floor of her bedchamber felt like ice against her feet and she hurriedly slipped into her stockings.

"Indeed, Miss, I've got the shivers myself," the abigail replied as she helped her mistress out of her bedclothes and into a summer dress. "You'll wear the cashmere shawl about your shoulders and be snug until the sun appears. Lady Chattering's, no doubt, got a throw in her carriage just the same."

"I wish Lady Chattering had not taken this sudden fancy into her head to visit Bognor Regis, or we should all be in our beds; lighting a fire is in the fore of my mind now, not waiting until the sun rises," Rosanna insisted.

"You'll be having a nice time, Miss. You'll not be moping around here no more," Betty assured her.

"And you'll have a respite from looking at me, too," Rosanna added, though she knew such a thought would not be on the faithful abigail's mind.

Rosanna let Betty coif her hair at the dressing table.

"At least I shall be away from London, a place I find wholly synonymous with Charles Cavanaugh

... the pink taffeta is so bright and cheerful," Rosanna commented on her maid's choice of gown, "perhaps wearing it will lift my spirits."

"And the parasol will be handy at the seashore," Betty added.

"The seashore—I still can not believe I am going. To tell true, I do not even remember Christina's having an Aunt Vilna. Well, it does not signify. All I have to know is that I am going and that my cases are ready. They are ready, are they not?"

"Of course. The groom has them below and will place them on the carriage as soon as it has arrived," Betty reassured her.

"Betty, you fuss so over my hair," Rosanna said impatiently, "Who will see me in the darkness of morning? Does it really matter that there is no great blush in my cheeks?"

"One never knows who one might meet. It will not do to have you arrive at Lady Chattering's aunt's house looking as though you just tumbled from bed."

"But I have just tumbled from bed, Betty!" she protested.

"But no one save you and I need know it," Betty defended her continued ministrations.

"I suppose you are right," Rosanna admitted and stopped her protestations.

She watched as the abigail coiffed her hair in a most becoming style, atop her head, with a cascade of curls falling about her shoulders. Betty put a dab of blush on both her cheeks and just a hint of pomade on her lips; they glistened in the light of the candle sorely needed in the darkness of the morning.

"I wonder that I should need the candle to

light my way to Lady Chattering's coach," she said and persuaded the abigail to escort her down the stairs and out onto the street when the carriage arrived.

Rosanna recognized Christina's groom, but only when he stood directly before her. There was such a fog that she could hardly see two feet in the distance.

"Is Lady Chattering within?" Rosanna asked.

"No, Lady Shelton. She was not yet down when it came time I was due here. We must return to fetch her," the man said as he helped Rosanna inside.

Betty poked her head in just enough to take the fox throw and place it on her mistress's lap.

"You shall be snug within the fur," Betty said before taking her leave. "Perhaps you can sleep until Lady Chattering joins you." She closed the carriage down and returned inside, rubbing her arms to keep the morning chill from her bones.

The carriage made a jostling motion as it crossed the streets of the sleeping city. Rosanna rested her head on her shoulder and thought she would fall asleep...

Rosanna felt the carriage stop abruptly. Could we be arrived at Christina's already? she asked herself. It seemed that she was only asleep for a moment. Rosanna thought little of it, nor of the voices she thought she heard outside.

"Is this Mr. Daniels' carriage?" Rosanna divined that a man asked, and laughed at herself for being so sleepy as to imagine this unlikely exchange.

When the carriage door opend, Rosanna fully expected to see her friend, but thought it so dark she would not be able to readily determine who sat on the other side of the leather seat. The carriage began moving immediately as the door closed.

"Good morrow," Rosanna said to her friend. "It is a boorish morning, is it not?"

"Indeed," said the voice of a man. "But is this some devilish trick Robert has played upon me?"

"If you have been tricked, we are equally deceived," Rosanna said, her heart pounding from fear. She could not be so asleep as to think she heard the voice of Sir Charles Cavanaugh. Who could this stranger be?

"I need not ask after the owner of so sweet a voice," Sir Cavanaugh said, at the other end of the carriage.

It was so dark that Rosanna could not make out his face unless she approached, but thought she saw the glimmer of those green eyes. "Can it be you, Charles?"

He moved closer. "My immediate question concerns where we are being taken. Do you know?"

"Only that I was to accompany Lady Chattering to Bognor Regis," Rosanna said, not knowing what else to answer, not daring to say that it did not concern her in the least, as long as they were together.

"A pleasant enough destination," he remarked with detachment. "But suppose we ask the groom?"

Sir Cavanaugh rapped on the glass partition repeatedly.

"He appears not to hear me," he said and noticed the great speed with which the horses fled from London, so as to discourage any sudden exit. "Do you suppose that our dearest friends took it into their heads to arrange this impromptu meeting?"

"It was not I who orchestrated this," Rosanna said defensively.

"I suppose not," he said, the iciness still in his voice.

"I am dreadfully sorry that you are to be inconvenienced in this way. I do not know what to suggest," she said, wanting desperately to throw her arms around him and never let go.

"We have simply to make the best of the situation. Whatever orders were given to the groom have certainly included that he must ignore us and anything we ask of him," Sir Cavanaugh said as he sat back, silent.

"Would it not be possible to enjoy ourselves?" Rosanna asked. "There is no reason to make this a worse adventure than it is already."

"To you, everything is an adventure, is it not?" He snapped suddenly.

"Charles—"

"No, everything is to be thought of in a light-hearted way, is it not? Even a proposal of marriage!" he insisted.

"That is not true. And if you would ever have allowed me to explain the true circumstances of our acquaintance—"

"And what would that signify to me?" he demanded to know.

"Though you might not speak to me again, you would learn that I do not treat everyone, nor everything, in so offhand a manner," she hurried to say before he could interrupt her anew.

"That matters little to me now," he said with forced disinterest.

"Perhaps I shall tell you anyway, as I have you a captive audience," Rosanna said, unwilling to believe that he could care so little for her so soon

'Before we met, I had little idea of what true love was like, much less faith that it even existed. I had convinced myself that I would never meet a man who would interest me half as much as my own pursuits did. And yet I felt that not being married stifled me in some way. I thought, erroneously, that the life led by such notables as Lady Wolverton and her circle was enviable, exemplary, and so what better match could I make than Irva Wolverton's own brother, a man whose company I found tolerable, if not pleasant. Our interests were compatible in the main, and where they were not, we would be left to our own devices. The Count and I had an understanding, a written accord to marry, no love, no false notions. We understood what we were doing.

"But then I met you, and I realized that marriage must be an alliance of two people who care for one another, not merely a convenient state of being. Of course, I should have told you about my understanding with the Count at the start. But I thought that you would think so ill of me that you would not even consent to be my friend. As fate would have it, whatever one seeks to conceal is always revealed in the most heinous way.

"Yes, I know even of your friends' wagering," Rosanna told him, "and so the knowledge came to you not only with pain, but humiliation as well. I can imagine your hatred of me, the worst kind of female, conniving, calculating, unscrupulous. But Charles," she said, leaning towards him, "if I panicked and lost all sense of reason, it was that I fell in love with you and was captivated by the magic in your voice, the intensity of your beliefs, by everything about you that caused me to question my own actions and thoughts. If you remember the note I sent you the night before you learned the truth, it was to confess this. But, of course, I was too late. And now I suffer that I have lost you at my own hand."

All the weeks of agony at not being able to say these words to Charles had left Rosanna beside herself. Now the misery flowed from her in her dialogue and she felt that at least the anguish at not being able to tell him how she felt was dissipating.

"Even though I lost you, Charles, I could not bring myself to marry the Count. I know now I cannot commit myself to another in the eyes of the Lord without truly desiring that inseparable bond. I do not expect forgiveness, only understanding and acceptance that I know better now, that the life led by Lady Wolverton is a sad substitute when the richness of love is absent. If it would please you, I would throw myself upon the mercy of the groom so that you might escape this unpleasantness."

Rosanna lifted her hand to knock upon the glass and Charles Cavanaugh seized it to hold to his chest.

"Do you not feel my heart pounding within me. It comes merely from our closeness. Did you really believe I could stop loving you as easily as I began? If I could not look at you, it was the thought of losing you again. Do you know that I began questioning my way of living as compared to that of Lady Wolverton, when it occured to me that my deficiency must have led you to seek out the Count even as I called upon you? Yes, I interpreted your secret as the cruelest form of betrayal—to not even tell me what was in your heart! But now I can well understand how difficult it must have been to have come so far along in your decision to marry only to discover that you could not go through with it. You must forigve yourself for what you did, for I do," he said, aware of the guilt she carried with her.

"You forgive me?" Rosanna asked, not believing her ears.

"How can I not, when I love you? And when you begin to forget the hurt and the upset of your error, we can begin building a life of our own—all that I ever wanted for us," Charles said as he took her in his arms.

Their embrace was jostled somewhat confusedly by the abrupt halt of the carriage. They looked outside and saw that the sun had indeed risen high in the sky, that they were far from London, in the countryside of a town neither could place.

The groom jumped from his seat and opened the door nearest Sir Cavanaugh. He waited to see what mood his passengers were in; he had been warned by Lady Chattering that they might not have reconciled. When he was satisfied that they were in good humor, he made the following, well-rehearsed announcement:

"Lady Christina Chattering, the Baronet Playmore and Mr. Robert Daniels invite Lady Shelton and Sir Charles Cavanaugh to enjoy a picnic breakfast in the country this morn in the hopes that it will contribute to their reunitement."

Rosanna and Charles applauded the groom as he produced a large basket of foodstuffs. He took the fur throw and set it upon a grassy mound.

"I will lay out the feast if you've both the appetite to enjoy it."

Charles turned to Rosanna, "Lady Shelton, might I request the honor of your presence at breakfast this morn?"

"Indeed," she said as she alighted from the carriage.

"And for every morn to come?" he asked as he took her hand.

"Yes, Sir Cavanaugh," she said with all the love in her heart, "for every morn to come."

THE BEST OF REGENCY ROMANCE
FROM WARNER BOOKS

YOUR WARNER LIBRARY OF
CAROLINE COURTNEY